"Dammit, Winnie."

He stopped and then spoke in a voice that sounded like rough steel. "I find you attractive. That complicates things." His eyes were impossible to read in the harsh shadows.

Suddenly her heart pounded in her chest. "Is that the truth?"

"Why on earth would I lie?"

His shocking candor made her want to be brave. And that desire gave encouragement to long-suppressed yearnings. Here was a man she wanted. And he wanted her.

"I find you attractive, too, Larkin," she whispered. "Very." Daringly she traced the curve of one sculpted biceps. His skin was warm to the touch. Arousal sang through her veins. Her gaze settled on his lips.

Larkin shuddered. "This can't happen."

"What?"

"This."

He pulled her into his arms and kissed her with raw desperation.

Dear Reader,

If you have children in your life, you know how their innocence touches your heart. My heroine, Winnie, is passionate about protecting those who can't protect themselves.

Into her house walks Larkin Wolff, a man who knows what it means to protect, but who also knows the pain that comes from failing those you love.

Winnie and Larkin are strong, self-reliant loners. Neither has managed to find a partner when it comes to romance. When they band together to provide a safe haven for the vulnerable ones, they fight a spark that is impossible to ignore. Sexual attraction leads to so much more, and they must decide if they can learn to trust each other.

I hope you enjoy their story!

Happy reading,

Janice Maynard

JANICE MAYNARD

TAMING THE LONE WOLFF

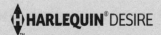

HARLEQUIN® DESIRE

Recycling programs
for this product may
not exist in your area.

ISBN-13: 978-0-373-73249-4

TAMING THE LONE WOLFF

Copyright © 2013 by Janice Maynard

Printed in U.S.A.

www.Harlequin.com

Books by Janice Maynard

Harlequin Desire

   The Billionaire's Borrowed Baby #2109
Into His Private Domain #2135
A Touch of Persuasion #2146
Impossible to Resist #2164
The Maid's Daughter #2182
All Grown Up #2206
Taming the Lone Wolff #2236

Silhouette Desire

   The Secret Child & the Cowboy CEO #2040

*The Men of Wolff Mountain

Other titles by this author available in ebook format.

JANICE MAYNARD

came to writing early in life. When her short story *The Princess and the Robbers* won a red ribbon in her third-grade school arts fair, Janice was hooked. She holds a B.A. from Emory and Henry College and an M.A. from East Tennessee State University. In 2002 Janice left a fifteen-year career as an elementary teacher to pursue writing full-time. Her first love is creating sexy, character-driven, contemporary romance. She has written for Kensington and NAL, and now is so very happy to also be part of the Harlequin Books family—a lifelong dream, by the way!

Janice and her husband live in beautiful east Tennessee in the shadow of the Great Smoky Mountains. She loves to travel and enjoys using those experiences as settings for books.

Hearing from readers is one of the best perks of the job! Visit her website, www.janicemaynard.com, or email her at JESM13@aol.com. And of course, don't forget Facebook and Twitter. Visit all the men of Wolff Mountain at www.wolffmountain.com.

For Stacy Boyd, editor extraordinaire!
I love working with you on each new project.
You are efficient and insightful, and you have a
genuine love for the romance genre. Your sharp eye
makes my stories shine. I think we make a great team.

One

Larkin Wolff stopped at the computerized video panel, pressed a button and showed his ID. After a brief pause, a light blinked green and the gate swung open. He passed through onto a long winding driveway constructed of almost pure-white crushed stone. Many of his clients surrounded themselves in acres of insulating property, but seldom had Larkin seen anything as peaceful and idyllic as the emerald fields, stately oaks and copses of weeping willows that lined the banks of a meandering creek.

Despite the sense that time stood still here, his skin tingled with a hint of warning. He'd built a career in high-tech surveillance, electronic security systems and even sophisticated cyber protection. Along the way, he'd developed what his siblings and cousins laughingly called a keen *Spidey sense*.

Larkin went along with the joke. Growing up on Wolff Mountain had made a man of him, and despite being a middle child with a troubled past, confidence was woven into his

DNA. But something about today's meeting made him itchy. And he didn't know why.

At long last, he pulled up in front of the house. The surrounding real estate, sprawling outside of Nashville proper, was home to country music legends, recording industry moguls and anyone else to whom money was no object. The two-story Georgian redbrick lady in front of him sat gracefully on the land, her many windows glistening in the afternoon sun.

Larkin grabbed a notebook and his laptop and got out, inhaling the scent of roses and freshly turned dirt. He had grown up in what many would call a modern-day castle, but this serene facade impressed even him.

Much of his work took him to city high-rises and aesthetically bland corporate headquarters. Today's setting would be a pleasant change. The summons had been a bit odd and non-specific. But perhaps he was imagining trouble where there was none. Families with lots of money often felt the need for protection. He should know.

Ringing the bell shaped in the head of a lion, he waited calmly. For a man in his occupation, patience was a prerequisite.

Suddenly, the large door swung inward and a woman stood before him. She was small, barely reaching his shoulder. Barefoot and wearing denim overalls cut off at the knee, the fabric neatly cuffed midthigh, she looked about eighteen. Her untamed hair was the color of corn silk, but it fuzzed out in a mass of unruly waves that almost overpowered her narrow face. Wary green-and-amber eyes surveyed him, even as her pointed chin lifted slightly. "Hello," she said, her voice low and melodic.

Larkin gave her a brief smile, trying not to notice that the thin white T-shirt beneath the overall bib seemed to indicate she was braless. The curves of her generous breasts peeked out the sides. "My name is Larkin Wolff," he said. "I'm here to see Ms. Winifred Bellamy. She's expecting me."

* * *

Winnie felt a sudden need for either smelling salts or a quick belt of whiskey. It had been a long, long time since a virile, handsome man had crossed this threshold. "I'm Winifred," she said, looking him up and down. "But please call me Winnie." She stepped back and waited for him to enter, leading him to the nearby salon.

It was one of her favorite rooms. She had furnished it simply but comfortably, and the small baby grand in the corner was one she played when there was no one around to hear. Audubon prints graced the walls, and a pale green silk Persian rug, enormous in length and width, cushioned her feet as she sank her toes into the pile. Its intricate pattern reminded her that someone, somewhere, had labored over its creation for days, months, years. Winnie admired such single-minded devotion.

She curled into an armchair and waved her guest to the sofa. "Thank you for coming so quickly, Mr. Wolff."

He shrugged. "Your note indicated some urgency."

"Yes." Fear and anxiety clenched her stomach, but she fought them back. She was not a victim. She was in charge. "I suppose you read the article I enclosed?"

He nodded with a grimace. "I did."

Winnie Bellamy hated being robbed. Money was one thing…she had plenty of it. But when *Arista Magazine* listed her as one of the twenty wealthiest women in America, Winnie lost something she valued more than anything else…her privacy…and her anonymity.

She placed her hands on the arms of the chair, deliberately displaying an air of confidence. "Where do we start?"

Larkin Wolff was not sure what she wanted from him. So he decided to push a little. If part of his line of questioning had more to do with sheer curiosity than actual necessity, well… that was his business. He settled back and drummed his hands on his knees. "Tell me about you and your family.... How did you end up on that wealthiest-women list?"

Ordinarily, he'd have opened his computer by now and would be making notes. But he didn't want to miss the nuances of expression that danced across Winnie's open-book face. Her posture and graceful movements projected dignity. She carried herself regally, as if she had spent her formative years at exclusive Swiss finishing schools. And perhaps she had.

She took a moment to almost visibly compose her thoughts before speaking. Her demeanor seemed pensive. "My parents had me when they were well into their mid-forties. The pregnancy was somewhat of an embarrassment to my mother. She and my father were academics, both with IQs off the charts. My 'accidental' conception made them look human, I think, and I'm sure they hated that."

"They are deceased?"

"Yes. Both had advanced degrees in anthropology and archaeology. Their careers and their marriage were spent crisscrossing the globe. They were much in demand as speakers at colleges, universities and basically anywhere that could rustle up the money to cover their exorbitant fees."

"And that's how they amassed a fortune?" He lifted a skeptical eyebrow.

"No, of course not. The money was always there. My mother's great-great-grandfather invented and patented some kind of engine during World War I, and my father's family owned a large publishing conglomerate in London."

"Where were you during all their travels?"

Trained to note small *tells,* he witnessed the brief moment her hands clenched on the chair arms before relaxing again deliberately. "I had governesses, tutors, semesters at boarding schools, an Ivy League education. Everything a child could possibly need."

"Except parents to tuck you in at night." The compassion

sparked by her terse narrative was born of his own dark memories.

"No," she said quietly. "I didn't have that. But there are worse problems, I assure you."

"Indeed. But having grown up myself without a mother and with a father who was all about business, I sympathize, Ms. Bellamy."

"I'd appreciate it if you would call me Winnie. *Ms. Bellamy* is too formal and, quite honestly, I hate the name Winifred. It makes me sound like an old-maid librarian."

He grinned. "You're far from that."

"I had you investigated, Mr. Wolff." Her cheeks were pink, and he was pretty sure his implied compliment had flustered her.

"I've got no problem there. You need to be able to trust who's doing your security work."

"Why is your firm called Leland Security? I would think using the Wolff family name would draw in clients."

"I have all the work I can handle, and besides…"

"Yes?" Her steady gaze dissected him.

"Well, in the beginning it was because I was a typical middle child. I didn't want to be overshadowed by my older brother or my cousins. Wanted to make my mark in the world. That kind of thing. Thankfully, I outgrew such posturing long ago, but I discovered in the meantime that if I was going to be handling discreet, sensitive matters, it made sense to fly under the radar. *Leland* is my middle name."

"Tell me, Mr. Wolff…"

"Larkin," he insisted.

"Larkin, then. Are you available for a large job? Do you have the manpower? The openings in your schedule?"

"Before I answer that, I have one last question of you. How and when did your parents die? Are you fearful for your personal safety because of the article? Is that it?"

She pulled her knees to her chest and wrapped her arms

around them. The childlike pose did nothing to detract from her natural beauty. Without a speck of makeup on her lightly freckled, ivory-skinned face, she reminded him of a young Meryl Streep. "My parents have nothing to do with this," she said tightly. "They were killed in a tsunami. At that time they were living with native peoples on one of the more remote islands of Indonesia. They never stood a chance."

"Were their bodies recovered?"

"Eventually. But there wasn't much left to bury. I had them cremated and flown home. DNA testing confirmed their identities. Lawyers aren't willing to turn over a billion-dollar fortune without definitive proof."

The horror of her tale was in no way minimized by her flat, deliberately emotionless recounting. Larkin had his own demons to battle, but here was a woman who knew what it meant to suffer.

"I'm sorry," he said quietly, wishing there was something he could do to ease the tension from her slight frame.

"It's been almost a decade," she said. She stood up and wandered the room, pausing to run a hand over the top of the piano. It was a loving gesture…sensual…appreciative. Without warning, his body reacted. He'd never met a woman less inclined to accentuate her looks, and yet Winnie Bellamy fascinated him.

"Do you play?" he asked.

When she looked up, it almost seemed as if she had forgotten his presence, so lost in the past as she was with memories. "For myself…on occasion."

"I'd like to hear you sometime," he said.

She pursed her lips. "Probably not."

"Why?"

She stared at him in silence, not deigning to answer his question. Perhaps she thought him impertinent. She turned and crossed the room to a small antique secretary. Pulling a silver skeleton key from her pocket, she unlocked the center drawer and extracted something he couldn't see.

When she returned to his side, she laid a piece of paper on the table at his elbow. His jaw dropped. Though his own personal financial portfolio was in the high seven-figure range (and that was not counting the portion of Wolff Enterprises that would be his in the future), it wasn't every day that someone tossed a check at him for half a million dollars. Though Winnie had signed the document, the *pay to* line was blank.

He picked it up gingerly. "What's this?"

She sat back down, this time crossing her legs and kicking one foot lazily. "That should cover everything I need from you. But I have to know that I am buying your utmost discretion. Nothing you learn about me or my estate can be shared."

There it was again, that tingling *Spidey sense*. He dropped the check. "I'm not a priest, a doctor, a shrink or, thank God, a lawyer," he said gruffly. "If you're involved in something illegal, I'll go straight to the police. You can buy my loyalty and discretion, but not a blind eye. Sorry."

She blinked, her pale lashes only a shade darker than her hair. "Wow. You shoot from the hip, don't you?"

"I won't take your money under false pretenses."

Winnie was not threatened by Larkin Wolff's displeasure. Instead, she was fascinated. When it was his turn to stand and prowl, she studied him. He was built like a baseball player, long and lean and athletic. Though his looks were pleasing, he wouldn't be called handsome. There was too much of a permanent frown line between his eyebrows and an unmistakable bump on the bridge of his nose that indicated a past break.

His eyes were a shade of steel-blue that could burn or chill given his mood. The man's body was a walking testament to working out, his biceps flexing beneath a thin dress T-shirt. He had removed a navy sport coat, and clad only in the oatmeal-colored knit, he looked powerful and intensely masculine. His short wiry hair was mostly black with a few strands of premature gray.

She knew from her files that he was barely thirty. But his visage and demeanor made him seem much older. "Sit down, Larkin. I can assure you that I am a law-abiding citizen." She was shocked to hear herself ordering him around—shocked even more when he obeyed.

His gaze locked with hers in unspoken challenge.

She sighed. "Since that article came out, I have been inundated with phone calls, packages and more than a few unwanted visitors. At one point, we even had to call in the bomb squad. Fortunately, it was a false alarm, but I can't endanger my staff's safety and well-being. I've received no less than six proposals of marriage, one of those from a convicted sex offender serving prison time. My personal email account was hacked last week, and the perpetrator sent pornographic images to everyone in my contact list. This has to stop…and soon."

Larkin leaned forward, his elbows on his knees. "I can take care of all of that for a fraction of your big check. Why so urgent? What aren't you telling me? Stuff like this blows over in a matter of weeks. New gossip arrives, fresh meat scents the air. In a month or two, I'm pretty sure you'll have nothing to worry about."

Swallowing the lump in her throat, she clasped her hands in her lap to keep them from shaking. "Even if I am overreacting, I have the right to hire you and ask for certain things… correct?"

There was that scowl again. "Of course you do. But part of my job is to advise you. And throwing away your money isn't necessary."

"I won't be throwing away a cent," she said, her throat raw with emotion. "For starters, I need you to do the obvious. Install whatever we need to guard our perimeter. And I want you to contract your people to be on duty 24/7 for an indefinite period of time."

"And deal with phone and internet issues."

"Yes."

"What else?"

She hesitated. Everything she had read about this man inspired confidence. But trust was not easily won for someone in her position. "I need you to fill out the check and accept it before we continue."

His eyes iced with suspicion. "I've told you. It's too much."

"Then I'll write two checks...one to Leland Security and one to a charity of your choosing. I want half a million dollars' worth of protection. Can you or can you not provide that for me?"

"Has anyone ever called you paranoid?"

She swallowed hard. "I don't imagine a man like you understands what it means to be physically vulnerable. Women are stronger than men in many ways, but we will always face the threat of an attacker's size and strength and come out on the short end."

"Have you felt physically threatened since the article ran?"

"No. But there are other issues. As soon as you are sure the house and grounds are secure, I want you to take me somewhere safe for a couple of weeks, three at the most. We'll leak the fact to the press that I'm running, but I'll be trusting you to make sure my bolt-hole is secure."

"I've got to tell you, Winnie. You're confusing me. And I don't like it."

She chewed her bottom lip. Larkin Wolff was not a puppet to be manipulated by her will. He had brains and brawn and a surprisingly keen intuition that told him she was lying, at least by omission. She could see it on his face. "Before we go any further, do I have your solemn promise that my personal life and affairs are to be guarded as zealously as my physical well-being?"

He didn't like being dragged by the tail in the dark. And he was pissed. A shiver worked its way down her spine. If he abandoned her, what would she do?

"Fine," he said curtly. "Top secret. Need to know."

"You're mocking me."

"Surely you understand that my employees will have to be kept apprised of any potential threats."

She didn't like it, but he had a valid point. The more people involved, however, increased the opportunity for exposure. "I understand," she muttered. "And I'm assuming you do thorough background checks."

He snorted. "What do *you* think?"

The impasse was clear, at least in her own mind. She needed Larkin Wolff. And the only way he could help her was if she trusted him with her sworn secret.

Abruptly, she stood up, feeling her knees go weak and her palms sweat. If she made a mistake, the consequences could be disastrous. "Follow me, please."

He rose, as well, his expression inscrutable. "Whatever you say."

The check still lay on the table. Trying to buy his silence had been a mistake. Larkin Wolff had a personal code of ethics that she prayed to God was the real deal.

When they made their way through the house to the back and out onto a cool, screened-in veranda, Winnie stopped and waited until he stood beside her, shoulder to shoulder. The view was pastoral, a warm spring day basking in a benevolent sun.

"Over there," she said, pointing until she realized her hand was shaking. She lowered it slowly. "That's my primary concern."

The building, a smaller version of the main house, sat the length of a football field away. Larkin studied it, his jaw rigid. "What's so special about that spot?"

Tremors shook her, making her limbs weak as water. So many people counted on her. She cleared her throat, tears burning her eyes. "It's a safe house for battered women and their children. Aside from a handful of trusted staff, myself and now you, only two other people know it even exists."

Two

Holy hell. Larkin struggled to reassess the mental picture he had painted of a slightly paranoid, vulnerable, eccentric rich woman. "You're not worried about your own safety at all, are you?"

Winnie never took her eyes off the house in the distance. "No. I can take care of myself." The stubborn tilt of her chin was an angle he recognized. Growing up, he'd seen it every day in one of his siblings or his cousins. An attitude that acknowledged life's unfairness, but a determination to spit in the wind anyway. Winnie continued, "It's my job to make sure those women and children stay out of harm's way. That stupid article has threatened the security I promised them."

"Why you? Aren't there sanctuaries in the city for abuse victims?"

She shot him a sideways glance. "Government shortcomings aside, such situations demand physical distance. Once we bring our clients here, it's much more difficult for angry husbands and boyfriends to track them down."

"So you deliberately court danger on your very doorstep."

She leaned back against a column, one bare foot tucked behind her as she balanced on the other. "You disapprove."

He shrugged. "Clearly you don't have the necessary precautions in place."

He could almost see her hackles rise. "We've never had a hint of trouble. Still haven't, for that matter…at least when it comes to my guests. But the article has opened a Pandora's box. I need you to nail shut the lid."

"I have to be honest with you, Winnie. You're damned naive."

Her eyes flashed and her hands fisted at her sides. "Maybe I wasn't clear. I'm hiring you for security, not judgment."

"Too bad," he said, the dual syllables terse. "My protection comes with a whole complement of advice. It's what I do." He looked out across the neatly mowed lawn. "Take me down there."

Winnie flinched. "Absolutely not. The women and children in the building are terrified of men…any men."

"I won't hurt them. Hell, I won't even scare them."

"You don't know that. Everything about you screams macho alpha guy. You practically ooze testosterone."

He grinned, the male in him reacting to her interest, even if it was reluctantly given. "Give me a little credit. I can do low-key. Part of my job is surveillance, remember?"

"I've never let anyone step over that doorstep except me and a handful of other professional women."

"Like who?"

"Doctors. Psychologists. A social worker." Her unease was palpable.

"You trusted me enough to hire me. Now let me do my job."

Their eyes locked, determination in his…enormous reluctance in hers. "Perhaps we could save that for tomorrow."

"*Now,* Winnie. There's no reason to wait." He hadn't yet had time to fully evaluate possible threats, but he needed to see the whole picture. Protecting the weak and helpless was a calling for him, perhaps not in his personal life, but definitely as a businessman. He would do everything in his power to make sure that Winnie and her charges were safe.

He kept his gaze steady, implacable. Sometimes people didn't understand how precarious their safety really was. He had a hunch that Winnie was fairly self-aware, but the notion that evil could strike at any moment was a difficult concept for most normal people to accept.

Larkin had seen things that chilled his blood, some of them in his own backyard. He never allowed himself to be lulled into complacency. The world was full of monsters, even on a day that seemed as lovely and serene as a midsummer night's eve.

At last, his dainty employer cracked. "Fine," she said, her expression irritated but resigned. "Let me get my shoes."

She was gone barely a minute. When she returned, something in his stomach tightened in appreciation. Her footwear was an odd cross between practical and quirky. Flat gold sandals made of an infinite number of narrow straps encased her feet and ran halfway up shapely, toned calves. The lick of arousal he experienced disconcerted him.

He swallowed, trying not to look down. "You ready?"

She lifted her chin, nose in the air. "Follow me." By her voice and expression he saw that she was determined to be in charge. Her contrariness amused him. He'd let her take the lead, but when it came to the job, he'd do it his way, even if she balked. Winnie was paying him for his experience and expertise. Whether she liked it or not, he would take care of whatever or whoever was causing problems.

The stroll across the lawn was accomplished without words. Birds twittered, wind rustled in the trees and somewhere in the distance a lawn mower hummed. Winnie, however, maintained a stiff-lipped silence. Once, when she stumbled briefly, he touched her elbow automatically. She jerked away, no surprise, but not before the feel of her skin was burned into his fingertips. Soft, warm…delicate. Focusing his attention else-where was surprisingly difficult.

All the while they walked, he scanned the area, catalog-ing deficiencies in her security. Unless she had some kind of electrical perimeter, the low split-rail fencing in the distance was nothing more than decoration. With her hand on the front door handle of the neat brick structure, Winnie paused. He saw her throat move as she swallowed. "The children haven't been able to play outside," she said, "since the article ran. And I'm responsible."

He saw pain in her eyes. Regret. Frustrated helplessness. All emotions he had known intimately as a child unable to protect his siblings. "You're not responsible," he said, touch-ing her shoulder briefly in what he told himself was a gesture of comfort. "The situation is regrettable, but easily fixed."

"What do you mean?" Hope and suspicion warred in her striking eyes.

"We'll string up a camouflage tarp tomorrow…the kind of thing they use on army posts in the Middle East. From the air no one will be able to see the kids."

"It's that easy?"

"Let's just say that's the least of our problems."

She worried her lower lip. "Promise you won't talk to them."

He mimed locking his mouth and tossing away the key. "Am I allowed to take notes?"

"Is it absolutely necessary? You strike me as the kind of man who keeps a lot of stuff in your head."

He grinned. "Whatever the boss wants."

Stepping through the doorway into a house full of women and children was not what he expected. Winnie had told him there were eight bedrooms and currently twenty-one clients. Instead of noise and confusion, an eerie silence reigned.

"Did they know we were coming?" he asked, sotto voce.

"They knew," she whispered. "Someone is always looking out the window."

Not a soul appeared to greet them.

Winnie took him room to room on the main floor. "We have an alarm that is set at nine each evening. It's programmed to ring in the house…my bedroom actually."

He frowned. "Not the police?"

"Things are pretty spread out around here, in case you haven't noticed. I guess you could say I'm the first responder."

"And what exactly do you think you could do?" he asked, not bothering to hide his incredulity.

Winnie stared at him with the haughtiness of a duchess. "I can shoot to maim or to kill, whatever the occasion demands. Don't worry, Mr. Wolff. I protect what's mine."

He felt his anger rise and had to swallow it back. "You've hired *me*," he said mildly. "No need anymore for you to mete out vigilante justice."

"You don't believe me." It was a statement, not a question.

He ran a hand across the back of his neck. "I'm not disputing your ability to handle a firearm. I'm merely suggesting you let me handle intruders from now on out."

"And how will you do that from the comfort of your swanky downtown office?"

"You know nothing about my office."

"Wrong," she said, her expression triumphant. "A trusted friend of mine made a fake appointment two weeks ago, met you and scoped out your operation."

"The hell you say…" His indignation mushroomed.

"It's not unethical."

"No, but it's…" He trailed off, unable to articulate the exact mix of emotions he felt. Had a man done the same thing Winnie had done, Larkin would have applauded his thoroughness. Then why was he so taken aback? "Am I allowed to know what your spy uncovered?"

She chuckled, correctly reading his pique. "He told me you ran a tight ship and that your offices indicated a healthy bottom line. Satisfied?"

Larkin shrugged. "I expected nothing less. That's all true." He turned away, determined to regain control of the situation. "I'll ramp up the security measures already in place, and I'll install cameras. With your permission, we can set up a monitoring station somewhere in your house."

"What happens when you spirit me away?"

"My best people will be on the job. I swear to you, Winnie, you'll be in good hands."

Winnie hoped she wasn't blushing. Her fair skin was a curse. Being in such close contact with Larkin Wolff was making her act like a flustered sixteen-year-old girl.

She shoved her hands in her pockets to keep them out of mischief. Larkin's broad shoulders and lean torso were made to cushion a woman's weary head. Winnie liked the idea, but depending on a man was dicey. It was one thing to *hire* a professional. That made sense in the most pragmatic way. But fantasizing about close contact on a daily basis shouldn't— couldn't—be allowed. Even if handsome blue eyes filled with keen intelligence were her own particular Achilles' heel. She'd predicated her life on being a good girl…on not rocking the boat. It was disconcerting to realize that she was suddenly contemplating the tantalizing benefits of being *bad*.

"I'd prefer that you not go upstairs," she said abruptly, trying to corral her hormones. "I don't want to upset my guests unnecessarily."

"I suppose it can wait." He appeared calm, but she picked up a vibe that said he was completely alert, ready to react in a split second to any sign of danger. A hundred and fifty years ago, he would have been the gunslinger seated in the corner of a saloon with his back to the wall.

All that intensity gave her the shivers. "What next?"

"I need to make a few phone calls, arrange for a security detail overnight while I'm getting other odds and ends set up.

And if it's not too much bother, I could use something to eat. I skipped breakfast."

She raised an eyebrow, mocking him. "The most important meal of the day? Maybe I should reassess my view of your abilities."

"Trust me, Winnie. I can run on coffee and sheer cussedness for days. Doesn't mean I have to like it."

Trust me. He tossed those words out as if they were the easiest thing in the world to do. Little did he know that her ability to trust was as corroded as an old car battery.

"Are we through here? The women will be wanting to start lunch, but they won't come down to cook while you're on the premises."

"Fine," he said. "Let's head back to your house and get this thing rolling."

Why was it that everything Larkin said sounded like a risqué comment? Perhaps it was the fact that Winnie lived like a nun…Mother Superior shepherding her flock. An asexual being, with nothing to show for her youth but a barrage of bad memories.

Maybe it was sacrilegious, but some days she had a hard time believing in a God who allowed little children to run in fear of their own fathers. It was a question greater minds than hers had wrestled with for centuries. And one that wouldn't be answered anytime soon.

Before she could lead the way back to the front of the house, a small head appeared around the edge of the doorway into the hall. "Hello, Miss Winnie. Who's that guy?" The child's stubby finger pointed accusingly.

"*Hola,* Esteban. *¿Cómo estás?*" She crouched in front of him. "This is Señor Wolff. He's working for me."

Esteban's dark-eyed gaze locked with Larkin's. "He doesn't *look* like *un lobo.*"

Larkin chuckled, mimicking her posture. He didn't try to touch the boy or get near him. Which told Winnie that he knew how to act around someone who had suffered at the hands of a violent loved one. "Wolff is my last name, Esteban. I'm helping Miss Winnie make sure this house is very, very safe."

"So my daddy can't find us and hit me and Mama again?"

Simple. Direct. And so very heartbreaking.

Winnie saw a muscle flex in Larkin's jaw. "That's right. I have lots of people who work for me, and our job is to keep you from being scared."

Esteban inched closer. "Do you have a gun?"

Larkin nodded. "Several. But I don't use them unless I have to. Guns are dangerous. Promise me you won't ever touch one until you grow up."

The child eyed him with increasing curiosity. "Okay." He looked at Winnie. "I wish we could play outside."

She grinned. "Mr. Wolff is going to help us with that, too."

Her assurance seemed to satisfy Esteban. She pulled him close for a quick hug. Many of the children didn't like to be touched, but this little rascal craved attention. And she was prepared to shower him with as much TLC as he could handle. "Go tell the ladies that Mr. Wolff and I are leaving. They can come downstairs and prepare lunch."

As she and Larkin walked back to the main house, he quizzed her. "So, the residents in your safe house basically take care of themselves?"

"Yes. I supply them with plenty of fresh fruits and vegetables. I have a standing order with the nearest grocery store for staples and the supplies for basic meals. It gives the women a sense of purpose and also the autonomy to feed their children as they see fit."

"Why?" he asked. "Why do you do this?"

The blunt question caught her off guard. She wasn't prepared to bare her soul to a man who was little more than a stranger. "It's the right thing to do. I have the money. I can meet a need. Lots of wealthy people are involved in charity work."

He opened the screen door to the veranda and held it for her as she stepped past him. "None I know go quite this far."

As she paused on the top step, almost eye to eye with Larkin since he lingered behind her, a harsh, familiar noise filled the air. "Hurry," she said, grabbing his arm and pulling him inside.

As they watched, a white-and-navy helicopter hovered overhead. They could clearly see the man who hung out one door, camera in hand. Despite the precariousness of his position, the daring photographer shot for several moments before saying something to the pilot. The vessel rose, made a wide circle and hovered again with similar results.

Winnie blinked back tears of helpless rage. "Can't someone arrest them? Isn't this illegal? Damn it, damn it, damn it. I hate this."

Three

Larkin shared her disgust. He touched her arm briefly, hoping to convey his concern and empathy. "Unfortunately, they aren't breaking any laws. But all he's getting is shots of buildings. Someone can write a story about your house, but with no photos of *you,* it won't make much of a wave in the gossip rags."

He felt Winnie's distress in the fine tremor that quaked through her slight frame. "I keep thinking they'll go away, but they don't. That's why I have to leave for a while." Her voice rose at the end, telling him that the stress of the past few weeks was reaching a breaking point.

"Your leaving is easy," he said, ushering her inside. With a sophisticated lens, someone could snap a decent picture even through the screen. But no need to court problems now. "You said you want me to take you away. I know a place so secure that no one will have a hope of getting near you."

She banged a pot on the stove with enough force to let him know she was still fighting mad. The soup she poured from a glass container was homemade if he didn't miss his guess.

"Where?" She glanced at him, a frown marring her finely etched features.

"Wolff Mountain."

The lid to the pot clattered onto the counter before she retrieved it and placed it with exaggerated care on the warming soup. "I've read about your family. They don't like outsiders mucking around in their business."

"It's my home. I can invite whomever I want. And I happen to know that no place within five hundred miles is as secure. I'll take you there, stay a couple of nights to get you settled and then you can consider the next few weeks a vacation in a mountain resort."

She wiped her hands on a dish towel and leaned back against the cabinet, her smile wry. "That's the most absurd thing I've ever heard."

"It makes perfect sense," he insisted. "Far more sense than finding an out-of-the-way location and paying round-the-clock staff to guard you. My sister, Annalise, is having a birthday party for her husband on Saturday. So I was planning on going to Wolff Mountain anyway. We'll circulate to the press a story that you're vacationing in St. Barts. The paparazzi will head south, and your house will be free of harassment. The story is bound to blow over while you're gone, and soon it will be safe for you to go back home, particularly with the added security my people will have installed."

"You came up with that plan in the last hour?" She cocked her head, studying him as if she were trying to see inside his head.

"The best plans are simple."

"It's not simple at all. Tell me, Larkin. Am I the type of woman you usually take home for a visit?"

She had him there. His typical encounters consisted of mutually satisfying sex with older women who weren't likely to want anything from him. Not married women. Never that. But women who were devoted to their careers and didn't want to put a lot of time into a relationship. In other words, female versions of himself. He opened her refrigerator. "You got any beer?"

"Answer me," she said.

He found an imported ale and popped the cap with the opener she handed him. "I think, with your permission, we'll tell my family the truth. I've never taken a woman to Wolff Mountain, so I don't want them getting any mistaken ideas. We have an abundance of newlyweds in my family. They are all nauseatingly happy. I'd prefer not to be the subject of speculation."

"I'd think that seeing all of your family content and settled would encourage you to follow suit."

"Not gonna happen." He took a long slug of his drink and sighed with appreciation. Nothing like an ice-cold beer on a hot day. When Winnie continued to stare at him in silence, he pulled a chair from the kitchen table, turned it around and sat down, arms resting on the curved wooden back. "I don't want to have to take care of anyone or anything but myself. Now that Annalise is Sam's problem, I choose not to answer to any woman. I'm a selfish bastard, I guess. But I like being footloose and fancy-free. Nobody looking to me for support, emotional or otherwise."

"And yet you spend your days taking care of people."

"That's different. That's my job."

Winnie didn't seem convinced. But she'd get the picture soon enough. Larkin was a lone Wolff.

She frowned at him. "I have the money to pay for a safe house *and* for round-the-clock security. I see no need to inconvenience your family."

"I don't believe in wasting money. Besides, with you at Wolff Mountain, I'll have no qualms about your safety. There's plenty to do. You won't be bored."

"I'm seldom bored. But this arrangement seems awkwardly personal."

"It's not ideal. I don't like blurring the lines between my

job and my personal life. But in this instance the benefits out-
weigh the negatives. Setting up a safe house anywhere would
take a significant amount of time—time you don't have. To
get you out of the situation immediately means going somewhere that's already secure. Plus, my family's home is close
enough to yours that we could get you back quickly in case
of emergencies."

Even as he spoke, warning bells sounded in his head. It was
disconcerting to realize how easily he dismissed them. Would
he have made the same decision if his client was less appealing? The answer was one he didn't want to face.

While she puttered around, putting soup in bowls, slicing
bread and setting the table, he studied her. Though she was
slight and graceful, she projected an air of capability that he
had to admire. Lots of people wrote checks to save the world.
Winnie walked the walk. He normally went for tall, leggy bru-
nettes. Yet somehow, in one oddly unsettling morning, he had
discovered that petite blondes with crazy hair and cat eyes had
the ability to get under his skin.

He'd tried his best not to stare at her breasts, even if they
did play an erotic game of peekaboo. It wouldn't do for him
to develop a "thing" for a client. When he took her to Wolff
Mountain, the reason would be business. Her safety. Nothing
more. He enjoyed her company, and the thought of spending
time with her for a couple of days was not unappealing. But
he wouldn't let himself get involved beyond that.

Larkin had learned a painful lesson early in life. You could
try to protect those you loved, but sometimes trying wasn't
enough. Too many failures in that arena had convinced him
that he didn't want a woman in his life on any kind of permanent basis. It was a smart decision, and one he stood by, even
today. Winnie was entertaining and stimulating. She would
make a suitable "plus one" for the party. Beyond that, they
were nothing more than business associates making the best

of a bad situation. Despite his undeniable attraction, he refused to have a temporary fling with a client.

Much like her looks, her cooking was unusual and satisfying. The shrimp gumbo she served him was unexpectedly hot as hell. As he choked and washed down his discomfort with a glass of water, she grinned. "Guess I should have warned you."

"You did that on purpose."

"You don't like it?" The mischievous look was unrepentant.

"Of course I like it. But now I'm forewarned."

"How so?"

"Never underestimate Winnie Bellamy."

He could tell that his dry comment pleased her.

She glanced at her watch. "As fun as this is, I've got things to do."

"I'm hurt."

"Be serious. Tell me what I need to know."

He stood and rolled his shoulders. "Give me an hour to make my phone calls and get one of my teams out here while I run back into the city and pack a bag."

"Pack a bag?" Her befuddled look amused him.

"I'm staying here until we leave for Wolff Mountain. Three nights. Think you can handle that?"

Her cheeks turned pink. "I'm sure it's not necessary for the head of Leland Security to stay on-site."

"You're paying me five hundred grand," he said laconically. "That bumps you to the top of the list."

"I'm sorry if I insulted you."

The mix of moss-green and muted-gold in her eyes mesmerized him. Despite her homespun attire, Winnie was alluring, seductive…perhaps most of all because he was fairly certain she had no clue how her looks affected the opposite sex. He thought her sideways glance was penitent, but then again, it might have been unconsciously sexual in nature.

Once more, he was perturbed by the way his body tightened

and his throat dried. He understood the mechanics of attraction. But it had never been an issue in a work setting. Which meant that he was treading unfamiliar ground. The uncertainty of his own responses put him on edge.

"We're good," he said gruffly. "I'll sit on the porch while I'm using the phone. I don't want to disturb you."

Winnie's gaze settled on his mouth, skipped down to his chest and dropped to the floor. "Make yourself at home," she said, turning away to gather dishes and tidy up. "I won't even know you're here."

Liar, liar, pants on fire. The old childhood taunt rattled around in Winnie's brain as she tried to tackle her usual afternoon chores. She had quite a few phone calls to make, as well. Not to mention preparing a room for her unexpected guest.

Her stomach fluttered with anticipation. She was used to living alone. Her staff came and went as needed. Mrs. Cross, her housekeeper and cook, normally worked nine-to-five, but she had the day off for a doctor's appointment. In her absence, Winnie wandered the upstairs hall trying to select a room for Larkin.

It wasn't an easy task. If she put him next door to her suite, he might get the wrong idea. But if she gave him quarters in the opposite wing, it could make her look like a prudish virgin, not to mention negating his ability to protect her.

In the end, she compromised—across the hall from her bedroom and two doors down. It was a masculine room done in shades of navy and umber. The king-size bed would accommodate his long frame, and the deep whirlpool tub in the luxurious bathroom was big enough for two people.

When her breath hitched in her throat, she knew she was in trouble. She would *not* develop a crush on Larkin Wolff. What a laughable idea. She was a lousy judge of men's motives, and she would rather run naked through a hailstorm before ever hinting at an interest in him. Though at times today the air had seemed thick and heavy with awareness, it was surely all on her side. Larkin Wolff was a professional, a remarkably handsome man in his prime. He could have any woman he wanted.

Winnie had neither the arsenal of feminine wiles nor the sexual confidence to see if the odd, quivery sensations she had experienced in his presence were one-sided. She was buying Larkin's expertise in security. Her life had been turned upside down by that stupid article, and she was determined to right it.

All I want from Larkin is protection. She repeated it over and over in her head, making sure she understood the score.

But when the doorbell rang at six o'clock, her thighs quivered, her breathing grew choppy and reality smacked her in the face. She was lying, especially to herself. Larkin Wolff would protect her and her charges from outside danger. But the absolute worst threat had already breached her defenses.

She was in sexual quicksand and sinking fast. Pasting on a smile as fake as a three-dollar bill, she swung open the door. "Back so soon?"

Larkin was hot, hungry and irritated with himself. He'd spent the past several hours trying to concentrate on business while at the same time spinning fantasies that involved a naked Winnie Bellamy in his bed. It was ludicrous. He'd like to blame the aberration on the heat or the fact that he'd broken his cardinal rule about drinking on the job and had a beer at lunch. Unfortunately, the temperature was still comfortably in the low eighties, and the alcohol content of the ale was minuscule.

So where did that leave him? He'd worked hard to keep his business life impersonal and his private life completely separate from business. As a security professional, he prided himself on protecting the weak, the innocent and, sometimes, the naive. Occasionally, he protected the powerful, if the price was right. But never, ever did he allow a client to break through his emotional firewalls. He was a man who liked his own company, and he didn't *need* anyone. More importantly, he didn't want *anyone* to need him…at least anyone who wasn't paying for his services.

Winnie, he could already tell, was going to pose a problem. He found himself making exceptions to hard-and-fast rules—going over and above what she had hired him to do—and he wasn't sure he could stop himself. Installing her in the bosom of his family made sense on paper. But the reality was far murkier. Would he have done this for anyone else?

When she opened the door, it was all he could do not to stare. She had showered recently. Her damp hair, twisted in a knot on top of her head, smelled of honeysuckle. He sucked in a sharp breath. *Down, boy.*

The overalls were gone, but now she wore soft, faded jeans that hugged her trim legs, along with a white T-shirt that read Take a Book to Bed. The image of his new employer tucked beneath the covers wearing who knows what sent his libido tumbling into an entirely inappropriate free fall. He cleared his throat, feeling heat creep up his neck. "I'm back."

She surveyed the small duffel bag at his feet. "So you are. Come in."

As he stepped into the cool foyer, he handed her a sack filled with paper cartons. "Chinese takeout. I hope that's okay. You said your housekeeper had the day off."

She grabbed the offering and inhaled. "Are you kidding? Ambrosia of the gods. I love living in the country, but the lack of fast food is a definite drawback at times. Come on into the kitchen. And by the way, you get points for paying attention. Most men I know would have missed that entirely."

"It's my job to notice details." Like the way her lacy bra barely concealed pert nipples pressing against thin fabric.

He dropped his bag at the foot of the stairs and followed her into the kitchen like a puppy dog sniffing for a treat. Her feet were bare. Though he had appreciated the sexy gold sandals, her naked toes with raspberry polish were equally alluring.

As they ate, Winnie's pointed questions reminded him that he was in residence as a professional.

She held up a chopstick, waving it in the air. "Let's hear it. What am I getting for my money?"

He grinned at her, enjoying the way she sparred with him. "Well, first of all, my top cyber guy is going over all your computer stuff via remote access right now. He won't tamper with any of your data, but he'll seal leaks and shore up weaknesses in your points of entry."

"I have no idea what that means in reality, but go ahead."

"First thing in the morning, I'll have a team here installing a sophisticated system around the perimeter of your property. It's a combination of fencing and electric sensors. I don't think you'll find it unbearably intrusive, but with the cameras and the monitoring station here in the house, my team can assure you that no one will approach unannounced."

When Winnie beamed at him, he felt the punch in his heart first and his gut second. Pleasing her could rapidly become an addiction.

"That's fast work," she drawled. "I'm impressed."

"During the next two days, I'll work with my team to make sure all the bugs in the system are ironed out. Then, with your permission, you and I will head out for Wolff Mountain first thing Thursday morning."

Her smile dimmed. "Are you sure you don't want to just stash me away with an assumed name in some anonymous city apartment?"

"Ideally, yes." Winnie's crestfallen expression pained him, but he plowed on. She might as well read his bottom line. "But I see no need to waste time, money and manpower when the solution is at hand without any need for preparation. As I said before, Wolff Mountain is a fortress. Because of that, I won't feel obliged to stick around. I have no qualms about leaving you there. You don't have to be scared of my family. They're pretty nice people, all in all."

"They're Wolffs."

"Yes. And you're Winifred Bellamy. Perhaps they'll be afraid of you."

That made her laugh. "I've never scared anyone in my life. I'm harmless."

"Says the woman who shoots to kill."

"Or maim."

"Do I get a choice?"

"Don't make me mad, and you won't have to worry about it."

They were flirting. He knew it, and he was pretty sure she knew it. The awareness in her eyes matched the ache in his groin. Such an unexpected turn of events could make his life both very complicated and extremely frustrating.

When he found himself watching her soft, pink lips form words while at the same noticing the gentle rise and fall of her breasts as she talked, he decided it was time to retreat until he could decide what to do about the situation. "I'm pretty beat," he said, with an exaggerated yawn. "If you don't mind showing me my room, I think I'll turn in and do some reading."

Her look of incredulity as she glanced at the clock made him squirm. Seven-thirty? She'd think he was some kind of geriatric. He backtracked quickly. "Of course, if you have any other suggestions…"

The room fell silent. His unwittingly suggestive add-on sounded far naughtier than he had intended.

Winnie eyed him curiously. "Like what?"

He swallowed. "Oh, I don't know. A walk. Netflix. Reality TV."

The heavy silence lengthened. Finally she responded. "An early night suits me, too," she said, her expression impossible to read. "I keep case studies on all my moms and kids, not as a licensed professional, but more of an anecdotal record while they're in my care. I'm behind on several of those, so I should catch up. Especially if I'm going to be gone for a few weeks."

Something struck him. "Does the state reimburse you for the expenses you incur?"

"Of course not. I *choose* to do this."

"Foster parents get a stipend."

"It's not the same thing at all. You know I don't need the money. I wouldn't take it even if they offered." She seemed offended that he would even suggest such a thing. Her motives for such dedication were unclear, but since she was only a client, he didn't press for more. As she stood abruptly, he followed suit. "I'll show you your room," she said, the words clipped.

Larkin followed her back to the foyer and up the stairs, pausing only to grab his bag. The house was furnished with impeccable taste, luxury in every detail, but nothing at all ostentatious. He wondered if she had redone the place after her parents' deaths, and he suspected she had. Somehow the decor reflected the personality of its owner.

When Winnie paused, Larkin followed suit, standing shoulder to shoulder with his hostess as he surveyed the room. He whistled. "Very nice." This close, he inhaled the scent of honeysuckle again.

"I hope you'll be comfortable. I appreciate your fitting me into your schedule. Let me know if you need anything at all."

There it was again. That pesky, subtle *does-she-or-doesn't-she* vibe that made his skin itchy and his sex twitchy. He edged past her, determined to remain in control. "I'm sure I'll be fine. We'll get started first thing in the morning."

Winnie stood in the doorway, arms spread frame to frame, expression pensive. "I'd better close the drapes," she said. "So the morning sun won't wake you." With rapid steps, she crossed the room. Now she stood dangerously near the bed. The enormous, hedonistic bed, covered in a brocade-and-satin comforter and sheets that were most likely soft as sin.

Larkin shoved his hands in his back pockets. "I'm always up early," he said, his throat like sandpaper.

Winnie hovered, straightening a knickknack, smoothing a

nonexistent wrinkle from the spread. "I'll have someone bring you coffee first thing. You're welcome to have breakfast here or in the dining room."

The longer she lingered, the harder he got. Hopefully, she didn't notice, because it wouldn't do for her to get the wrong idea. He had never allowed his professional life and his personal life to intersect. Even though taking Winnie to Wolff Mountain made sense, and even though he would be the one taking her there because it was *his* family, he had never had a relationship with a client, and he wouldn't start now. "I'll be fine, Winnie. Good night."

Her face fell as she registered his clear dismissal. "Okay, then. I'll see you tomorrow." It took everything he had to watch her leave the room and not stop her. When she was gone, he sank down on the bed, head in his hands. He'd never taken on a case he couldn't handle. This couldn't be the first. He wouldn't let it.

Four

Winnie was aroused. As ill-timed and unusual as the symptoms were, she recognized them. Her skin was damp, her thighs trembled and the butterflies pitching to and fro in her stomach weren't from nerves. She *wanted* Larkin Wolff. This was a complication she had never anticipated when she set out to hire a security expert.

She'd been so upset in recent weeks about the stupid article that she hadn't allowed herself to remember the past. Now that omission came back to haunt her. What did she know about men, after all? One nasty encounter just after her parents' deaths had put her emotions into deep freeze. She didn't *want* to feel like a sexual being. Acknowledging such vulnerability scared her to death.

Though Larkin was here to protect her, some deep survivalist instinct told her he was dangerous. And yet, paradoxically, that very danger called out to her. Suggesting that she might abandon her lifelong persona as a good girl and throw caution to the wind.

The evening passed with agonizing slowness. She was uncomfortably aware of Larkin's presence mere steps down the hall. So accustomed was she to being alone in the house at night, she was distracted by the novel sense of companionship. After a couple of hours of legitimate work, as well as sixty minutes of guilty-pleasure TV, she took a shower and prepared for bed.

Though she had not heard a single sound from Larkin's suite, his presence was loud. She imagined him walking around the room…or reading…perhaps stripping off his clothes and letting them lay where they fell as he strode into the bathroom and ran water in the Jacuzzi. Imagining a naked Larkin Wolff was not conducive to sleeping.

It was a cool night with no air-conditioning needed. But her skin was hot to the touch, and perspiration dampened her pillowcase. Grumbling at no one in particular, she climbed out of bed and flung open a window, leaning out to inhale the fresh, scented night air. At last, with the lacy sheers swaying in a light breeze, she returned to her bed and fell into a restless slumber.

Sometime around 2:00 a.m. the gentle beep of the alarm at her bedside went off. She jerked awake, fumbling to glance at the readout. Probably nothing more than a bird or squirrel on a windowsill. It had happened before. But she always checked. Always. Because she knew firsthand what it meant to be scared and helpless. She'd made it through her own dark days unscathed. Thank God. And that deliverance gave her a moral imperative to pay it forward.

After shoving her feet into flip-flops, she grabbed her gun from its hiding place, tucked a small flashlight into her pocket and tiptoed down the hall. Larkin's quarters were silent. No hint of light beneath the door. He was probably sound asleep.

For one brief moment, she contemplated waking him. After all, she had hired Larkin to deal with intruders. But the alarms were extremely sensitive and often went off for no good reason. It would take her only minutes to dash down to the safe house, do a quick reconnoiter and come back to bed. Besides, the thought of waking Larkin made her shiver. Seeing him all sleep-rumpled and sexy might be a temptation she'd rather not face.

She wasn't stupid, though. If anything at all looked danger-ous or out of place, she'd back off immediately and get him to help her.

The grass was chilly and wet against her toes. She moved quickly but silently, sure of the familiar terrain. Overhead, the Milky Way arced its way across the sky, peopled with a bil-lion stars. It was a night for lovers and romance. But as usual, she was alone.

When she reached her destination, she slowed, listening intently. Only if someone actually opened a window or door would the residents be awakened. Otherwise, Winnie dealt with the nuisance of the very sensitive alarms. Once, a ground-hog had begun chewing through one of the wires, and all hell had broken loose. Even now, she remembered in vivid detail the looks of sleep-muddled terror on the faces of women and children in her care.

She moved covertly, fairly certain no danger lurked, but taking precautions, just in case. As she neared the back of the brick house, a shadow melted into the darkness. She froze. Was she seeing things, or had someone actually moved?

The mournful hoot of a nearby owl made the hair stand up on her arms. In the darkest hour of the night, it was easy to let an active imagination run wild. With her hand fixed on her gun, she inched her way forward. The safety was on. She wasn't stupid. But she could get off a shot quickly if she needed to.

She took one more step. In an instant, hard masculine arms came around her from behind, her gun was wrestled from her grip and a big hand clamped down over her mouth. Her muf-fled scream was nothing more than a whisper in the night. She fought wildly, trying to free her arms.

What must have been only seconds played out in agonizing slow motion.

And then a very familiar voice rumbled at her ear. "Shut up, damn it. You'll wake the whole house."

Her body went limp in relief. Larkin dragged her like a rag doll to the garden shed at the rear of the building. Pulling her inside, he shut the door and yanked the chain to illuminate a single lightbulb, all the while cursing a blue streak as he checked the safety on her gun and laid it aside.

He glared at her. "What in the hell are you doing?" he demanded, veins standing out in his neck. "I could have killed you."

Fury replaced the knowledge that she wasn't in the hands of an ax murderer. "The alarm went off in the house. I told you I'm the one who checks on it."

His eyebrows rose to his hairline. "You hired *me*. Remember?" The thumb he jabbed toward his chest emphasized his anger.

Where did he get off chastising *her*? "I didn't know you were prowling around."

"I told you I'd take care of things."

"Tomorrow. You said tomorrow." They were both yelling in hoarse, muted syllables that nevertheless escalated in volume.

He scraped his hands over his head. "My team is already here. We were running some preliminary drills to see how much we have to do to lock this place down."

"You should have told me. You should have introduced them. These women and children are *my* responsibility. I won't be kept in the dark." She was so mad, she shoved him in the chest. It was like pushing against granite. Yanking her hands back, she wrapped her arms around her waist, trembling wildly.

Larkin stared straight at her, remorse in his gaze. "You're right," he said softly. "I should have. It won't happen again. In my defense, none of my clients has ever been as invested in the process as you are. I'm sorry I didn't keep you informed."

His genuine contrition deflated her indignation. "Was it you who set off the alarm?"

He nodded. "Probably. To be honest, I assumed you had turned off the monitor in your bedroom now that I'm here. I was intent on bringing my people up to speed or I would have mentioned it."

Adrenaline winnowed away, leaving her spent and shaky. "I thought you were going to sleep."

"I said that to get away from you."

A lump lodged in her throat. "Charming."

"It's not what you think."

"What am I supposed to think?"

"Damn it, Winnie." He stopped, ground his jaw and stared at the floor. Finally he spoke in a voice that sounded like rough steel. "I find you attractive. That complicates things." His eyes were impossible to read in the harsh shadows.

Suddenly the oxygen in the shed evaporated. "Is that the truth?" Her heart pounded in her chest. *Danger. Danger. Danger.*

"Why on earth would I lie?"

His shocking candor made her want to be brave. And that desire gave encouragement to the long-suppressed yearnings of Bad Winnie. Here was a man she wanted. And he wanted her. Reluctantly, but still... Her heart raced. "I find you attractive, too, Larkin," she whispered. "Very. Attractive, I mean." Daringly, she reached out and traced the curve of one of his sculpted biceps. His skin was warm to the touch. Though the night was cool, Larkin was wearing a short-sleeve polo shirt that stretched to accommodate his hard, taut body.

His stood rigid as she ran her fingers from his shoulder to his elbow. Arousal sang through her veins and urged her on. Her gaze settled on his lips. Being a good girl all the time was no fun at all. Desperately, she wanted to taste him. But at what cost?

Larkin shuddered when she used her thumb to trace the bend of his arm. "God help me," he groaned. "This can't happen."

"What?" She couldn't make sense of anything. Not now. Not in the middle of the night when the world seemed strange and conducive to madness.

"This."

He yanked her into his arms, his big body enfolding her smaller one like a warm blanket. She felt his taut rib cage, noted the ridge of his belt buckle digging into her skin, heard the shallow rasp of his breathing. His mouth took hers unapologetically. No buildup, no foreplay. Just a raw desperation that layered confusion upon desire and dragged a whimper from her starved lungs.

When she communicated her need to breathe, he moved his attention to her throat, her collarbone. Her sleepwear consisted of a silky camisole and thin knit boxer shorts. When one of his big thighs pressed between her legs, her knees wobbled. He held her with one hard arm across her back as he ravaged her fevered skin.

"Larkin…"

"Hmm…"

"I thought I was the only one."

"God no." His teeth grazed her nipple.

She jerked, struggling to get closer, or maybe to get away. Who knew? Her hands found their way to the back of his head. Playing with the short hair at his nape, she felt reality dissolve in sheer, animalistic hunger. "I don't even know you."

His laugh held little humor. "We're getting closer by the second. Shut up and kiss me."

Obeying seemed like the best course of action. One of his hands had found its way down inside the elastic waistband of her sleep shorts and caressed her bare bottom. "You're so damned soft," he groaned. He squeezed her ass cheek.

She felt his arousal, huge and hard at her belly. With a house full of delightful bedrooms at her disposal, she was chagrined to find herself searching wildly for a horizontal surface in the tiny enclosure filled with potting soil and manure.

"I don't think this is going to work," she groaned.

At that instant, a two-way radio in Larkin's pocket generated static as a disembodied voice intruded. "Hey, boss. Where are you?"

Larkin froze. A heartfelt curse echoed her own sentiments. He released her so abruptly she stumbled. "I'm behind the house," he said, the words terse. "Don't move. I'll come find you."

The radio went silent. Winnie hated the harsh glare of the unadorned overhead lightbulb. She felt naked, exposed. Larkin looked nothing like a romantic hero. His tight expression fell halfway between sexually frustrated and pissed.

"Well, this is awkward," she said, attempting humor to dislodge the giant boulder crushing her chest. "I'll leave you to it." Her eyes stung with tears she would never in a million years allow to fall. Larkin was a guy. He'd grabbed her half-clothed body, and the predictable had happened. End of story.

He didn't have to know that such raw passion was foreign to her. That it had been years since she had felt more than a mild interest in the opposite sex. That he was the first man in a decade to coax her into bestowing her trust.

Grabbing the chain in a wild attempt to disguise her chaotic emotions, she plunged the shed into darkness and slipped out the door. Larkin was right on her heels, his breath hot on her neck. "Not so fast, Winnie. We have to talk."

Her choked laugh held more than a hint of hysteria. "Isn't that my line?"

He shook her gently. "I shouldn't have kissed you."

Wow. The pain that statement invoked was far out of proportion to the fact that she had met this man only a day ago. "Well, we're even, then," she said, her words deliberately flip. "I shouldn't have kissed you either." Unable to hold her tears at bay despite her best efforts, she fled.

* * *

Larkin let her go. He'd botched this job so badly he was amazed she hadn't fired him on the spot. First he'd overlooked the glaringly obvious fact that his new boss expected to be consulted at every level. And then he'd compounded his gaffe by kissing her senseless. Good Lord…

Remembering the feel of her in his arms hardened his sex to the point of pain. Hunger raged in his veins even now. Had his employee not intruded, Larkin would have lifted Winnie into his arms and taken her standing up. The rush of crazed passion was something he hadn't experienced since his hormonal college days.

But Winnie was no sorority girl looking to add notches to her bedpost. She was a fascinating, complicated woman. A female for whom he felt a visceral, inexplicable need. Such wild emotion was not to be trusted. He was being paid to keep her and her flock safe. In those brief moments when he'd kissed her and felt her small, perfect body meld to his, he'd had no thought at all for his job.

The realization stunned him. Was he kidding himself about his reasons for suggesting Wolff Mountain as a hidey-hole? He no longer allowed any woman to influence his decisions. At least not since his little sister married Sam. Larkin, for the first time in his life, felt free.

So why complicate his life?

Without warning, he stubbed his toe on an unseen rock in the grass. The dull pain shocked him back to reality. Screw self-examination. Taking Winnie to the mountain was expedient and well thought out. It had nothing to do with sex.

An hour later, with his crew safely on alert and all initial summations complete, Larkin strode back up the lawn toward Winnie's house. He already knew which windows were hers, and they were dark. He let himself in, locked the doors and moved wearily up the stairs, his tread virtually silent. In the upstairs hallway, he paused, his hand on the doorknob to his room.

Why had she kissed him back? Had she merely been humoring him? Or was she starved for male companionship? She poured her heart and soul into her cause. Did that leave any time for relationships? Her fire and boldness in the shed had surprised him and made it much more difficult to stop thinking about her in inappropriate ways.

He showered rapidly, not wanting to think of who and what lay so close at hand. If he went to her room, would she welcome him?

Beneath the covers, he sprawled naked and still damp, waiting for the thundering of his heartbeat to calm so he could sleep. Suddenly, the idea of taking her to Wolff Mountain seemed fraught with pitfalls. He knew the correct angle to take with Winnie. Practical and businesslike. If he allowed himself to break his own personal rules, he would only end up hurting her.

Larkin had no plans for matrimony. Ever. He'd seen a dysfunctional marriage close at hand, and it had tormented him, even if the whole thing had been over before he started school. Remembering the panic, the fear, the driving urge to protect his siblings, sent nausea roiling in his belly.

He liked being on his own. And Winnie Bellamy was not the kind of woman to let herself be used and tossed aside. She was a class act and deserved a man who would cherish her.

Spilling the Wolff Mountain plan without thinking it through was unlike him. He was seldom impulsive, though his ability to make snap decisions might seem so. Taking her to Wolff Mountain was unconventional, but expeditious. No fuss, no time commitment. He'd drop her off, enjoy the party and be on his way. If he changed the plan now, he would undoubtedly hurt her feelings. She had a backbone of steel when it came to protecting what was hers, but in her beautiful eyes he saw a wariness that was surely born of pain.

He didn't want to be the man who hurt her. If sexual insanity was all he had to offer, surely it was best to back off. She'd responded to him like a flame set to dry tinder. Not by word or expression had she indicated that his kiss was unwelcome. And he knew women's bodies well enough to know when pleasure was given and received.

Simple sexual attraction could be ignored. But the danger he faced was that something about Winnie called to him. He saw her waifish vulnerability and wanted to protect her. To shelter her. That was why he had to stay away. Because he had failed too many people in his life already.

At long last, he felt drowsiness claim him. He didn't need a woman in his life. He was happy with his freedom. Sexual satisfaction was available to a man like him in many ways. It was better for everyone if he kept his hands off Winnie.

Five

A lousy night's sleep made for a rough start to Larkin's day. And it went downhill when he found out that Winnie had made a run for it. The pleasant housekeeper shared the information that *Miss Winnie* had gone into town to run errands.

Larkin seethed as he went about his work. He was worried about his brand-new client with the crazy blond hair and the pointed chin. And what bothered him was that the worry felt personal. Intimate. Because of that, he reminded himself she was a grown woman. He did his best to put his worry aside and focus on securing her estate and the safe house. The Bellamy property was crawling with Leland Security employees. Pretty soon, not even a gnat could infiltrate the place without an alarm going off. Larkin also had plans to station female techs in the safe house on rotating shifts. He wanted someone inside 24/7 as a precaution. But that would have to be subject to Winnie's approval. In the meantime, until she decided to come back, all his people had orders to stay away from the brick building that housed Winnie's hidden population.

By five o'clock, Winnie still hadn't returned. The house-keeper departed with instructions about dinner. All of Larkin's day-shift people went off the clock except for the team guarding the perimeter. Larkin had worked his ass off for hours. He was hot, tired and disgruntled.

Though most people would say it was a tad too early in the year for swimming, he'd taken note of the small but beautiful pool in the backyard of the main house. When he drew back the solar cover, the water gleamed pure and welcoming. Someone had already cleaned and treated it for the upcoming season.

The temptation was too great. Larkin stripped out of his khakis and work shirt and dived in, wearing nothing but a pair of circumspect navy boxers. No one was around to see him, so what did it matter? He ran through a set of punishing laps, glad for the exercise, relishing the cold water and determined to clear his head.

When he finally climbed out, he realized that he hadn't thought to bring a towel. The sun was still warm, so he dragged a lounge chair until it faced west, stretched out and closed his eyes. An alien feeling of contentment washed over him as the sun's rays dried him.

Birds twittering in the trees lulled him into sleep.

Winnie was aggravated with herself. Not only had she wasted an entire afternoon roaming around Nashville wearing an uncomfortable wig and dark glasses, now she was afraid to go home. The morning's agenda had included legitimate business. A meeting with her Social Services contact. A stop at a furniture store to see about more bunk beds for the little ones. A much-needed foray into the women's-wear department at her favorite store.

Buying clothes for herself was not something she thought of very often. She didn't go anywhere to need much more than jeans and tops. But at Wolff Mountain, she'd be expected to dress in a certain fashion. She didn't want to embarrass either Larkin or herself.

Fortunately, she knew what she liked and what suited her. The saleslady recognized her, probably from her signature, and asked about the article. She was pleasant, though, and Winnie didn't get the impression that she was going to run to the phone and summon the press. Maybe Larkin was right and this whole "richest women in America" thing would blow over soon. But in the meantime, Winnie still had her guests to think about. Their safety and well-being.

With a platinum credit card smoking, she loaded her car with boxes and bags. After lunch at a trendy tearoom, she should have headed home. But the thought of facing Larkin was so distressing, she literally couldn't point the car where it needed to go.

As she drove at random, appreciating the display of azaleas, daffodils and lilacs in the suburbs, she pondered what to do. One option was to pretend nothing had ever happened. Let last night seem like a crazy dream. Surely Larkin would play along.

Avoidance was another tack. Today being a case in point. But she had things to do at her house, and even though the property was substantial, hiding out wasn't an effective choice.

Then again, she could walk right up to Larkin, kiss him square on the mouth and invite him to her bedroom. That brash action might have more appeal if he was leaving anytime soon. Instead, the plan called for her to accompany him to Wolff Mountain. Which meant a certain amount of togetherness.

And if she propositioned him beforehand and was politely rejected, she didn't think she'd have the composure to carry out an extended visit on his home turf. She glanced at her watch and groaned. Time to face the music.

When she parked the car in the garage and tiptoed stealthily into the house, she was greeted by nothing but silence. Fabulous smells wafted from the kitchen, indicating that Mrs. Cross had left dinner in the oven. No sign of Larkin and no evidence that he had already eaten.

She climbed the back stairs and made her way toward his bedroom. One quick peek showed a neatly made bed and no sign of human habitation. Where was he?

For one brief, stomach-curling moment she wondered if he had left. Quit the job. Moved on. But no. Whatever his personal inclinations, he would not have left her high and dry. Though it was possible he had passed off the responsibility to some-one else after that kiss. The wave of disappointment brought on by that thought told her she was in big trouble.

When her stomach growled, she decided she might as well eat without him. It was a beautiful evening, so she carried a cotton place mat and some silverware out onto the veranda, intent on setting a small table before she served her plate.

Then she spotted him. Out by the pool, sprawled like a demigod on her rattan lounger, lay Larkin Wolff. He must not have heard her drive up, because his large body, sculpted with muscles, didn't move.

What was he wearing? From this distance he might as well have been nude for all she could tell.

What was she going to do? Eat alone? Skulk up to her room and hide out until tomorrow?

Nibbling her lower lip, she came to a decision. She was a grown woman in charge of her life. A fairly lonely life, by some standards, but a life she had crafted to please herself. She was not afraid of Larkin Wolff. In fact, it was entirely possible that she might work up the courage to seduce him while she had the chance. Not too many men crossed her path these days, and certainly none who looked like Larkin.

Unfortunately, she'd misread a man's motives once before and had lived to bitterly regret her actions. If she threw her-self at Larkin, banking on a mutual attraction to ease the way, it was entirely possible that he would shoot her down. He had made it very clear that he didn't mix business with pleasure. But he had kissed her. So what did that mean?

The reverse was also dangerous. What if he gave in? What if they indulged in wild recreational sex? What if she couldn't protect herself and made the mistake of becoming emotionally involved? She had survived multiple tragedies in her life. Losing her head over the intense, charismatic Larkin Wolff could add to that list. Even if she told herself she could keep things fun and easy, the fact of the matter was…she was not a woman who took physical intimacy lightly. For a lot of reasons.

She wished she could seduce Larkin and not worry about the consequences. But she wasn't made that way, despite the recent appearance of Bad Winnie. So her only option was to keep her emotional distance.

On shaky legs, she walked out to the pool. Most days lately the groundskeeper had taken off the cover to let the water begin to heat. But in truth, it took a string of near-ninety-degree afternoons to warm the water to Winnie's comfort level. And they weren't there yet. Larkin must be made of sterner stuff.

She paused a few yards away from her quarry. Now she saw the pile of discarded clothing. Her face heated to scalding as she realized he was wearing nothing but his underwear. Other than the fabric, it wasn't all that different from a pair of swim trunks. But witnessing the unmistakable shape of Larkin's resting sex made her stomach feel funny.

Drawn by curiosity, she inched closer. He had been up much of the night, so it stood to reason that he was exhausted. His broad chest rose and fell with deep, measured breaths. Dark lashes hid his beautiful blue eyes. Even his legs and feet were sexy.

Though her hand trembled with the temptation to wake him, she began to back away. Unclothed, he seemed far more intimidating and dangerous than he had before. She was out of her league. Way out.

As she moved away quietly, he sat up, rested his hands on his knees and rolled his neck. "Like what you see?"

His lips curled in a taunting smile that dared her to pretend she hadn't been staring. Their gazes met, clashed. She was the first to look away. Taking a deep breath, she faced him with a determined smile. "Dinner's ready. I thought you might be hungry."

"Where have you been all day?"

"Out."

"I thought you were worried about your tenants."

She shrugged. "I knew you were standing guard."

"And what about your own safety?"

"I used a disguise. Besides, I can go most places without being recognized. It's only a problem here, because people now know where I live. The magazine spilled that information without my permission."

He stood, picked up his pants and stepped into them, zipping and buckling as if it was the most natural thing in the world. "I think you were avoiding me."

Her face flamed with color, either from his pointed reference to last night or because his bare chest made her woozy. "What a ridiculous idea."

He didn't bother putting on the shirt. Perhaps because he knew his half-dressed state gave him the upper hand. "Are you just going to ignore it?"

"Ignore what?"

He snorted in disbelief at her deliberately obtuse answer. "Our kiss."

"That's my plan." One she hadn't firmed up until just that moment.

"I didn't peg you for a coward."

The accusation stung. But she wouldn't allow him to goad her. Not when she felt so ill-prepared for the fight. With all the self-possession she could muster, she turned her back on him and walked toward the house. "You're welcome to eat with me on the porch." She tossed the words over her shoulder, not looking to see if he would follow. "But put on a shirt, because we dress for dinner."

Larkin grinned in spite of himself. Winnie Bellamy was a pistol, as his uncle Victor used to say. Truth be told, Winnie would no doubt fit in well with the outspoken, arrogant Wolffs. She was soft in appearance and speech, but beneath her careful etiquette and creamy magnolia skin was a woman with a lot of passion. For her life's mission, for her home and, judging by last night, for one lucky man who had the guts to take her on for the long haul. Too bad Larkin wasn't that man.

He lingered a moment to put on his shoes and button his shirt. By the time he reached the porch, Winnie had brought out two plates of steaming lasagna along with a bowl of salad. Larkin's stomach growled audibly as he ascended the steps. "Smells great," he said, opening the screen door and surveying the cozy tête-à-tête she had arranged.

For the first time he realized she was dressed up. A taupe linen shift dress. A necklace of jet beads that nestled between her breasts. And matching stud earrings. Her strong-willed hair had been tamed into a chignon at the back of her neck. Today she looked every inch the heiress.

But her feet were bare. And that made him smile.

She sat down and waved a hand. "Don't let it get cold."

They ate in companionable silence as the shadows lengthened. Perhaps Winnie would have been content to let the meal remain so, but his curiosity got the best of him. He sat back, sipping the glass of Chianti she had offered him. "I'm still puzzling over this thing you do, Winnie. Did you have an unhappy childhood? Do you see yourself in those kids down there?"

She seemed shocked by his question. "Good Lord, no. My parents were lovely people. Even if I had drawn crayon murals on the walls and danced naked at one of their dinner parties, they would never have used corporal punishment. They doted on me in their own way. But they simply didn't know what to do with a child. They could have offered me up for adoption, you know…or even terminated the pregnancy. I've always been grateful that they wanted me, even though I was a complete disruption to their ordered lives."

Larkin heard the truth in her words. And he knew she had never been married. So what compelled her to reach out to battered women and frightened children? Normal people weren't random in their actions. Everyone had an angle, something that drove them. Larkin was determined to find out Winnie's motivations. Why it was so important to him, he couldn't say.

When it grew too dark to see well, Winnie spoke quietly. "I need your help tomorrow," she said. "I have to tell everyone in my care that I'll be leaving Thursday. I want you to talk to them…explain that they're safe. And that with me gone, the harassing helicopters and strange people trying to access the property will stop."

"I thought I was persona non grata."

"I'll go in first. Prepare the way. But they will be okay. There's something about you that inspires trust. You may be physically strong and capable, but you would never hurt someone defenseless."

"How can you be sure?" He was genuinely curious.

"I don't know exactly. I suppose I could be wrong. But you seem like a protector to me."

He thought of all the nights he had hidden little Annalise in his bed, her small body quaking as they both cowered from their mother's angry shouts. Larkin had always been torn. His brother, Devlyn, was bigger, stronger. Larkin heard the blows and knew his sibling would never cry out. He wanted to run out into the hallway and hit his mother until she backed off. But someone had to protect Annalise.

So Devlyn faced the alcohol-fueled beast on his own. And Larkin bore the shame.

He shifted restlessly in his chair. Rarely did he allow the

memories to intrude. But Winnie's artless assessment of his character brought it all back. "It's true that I would never harm anyone weaker than I am. But don't paint me as a hero, Winnie. I can be as self-serving as the next guy."

He helped her carry the dishes to the kitchen. The lights in the house seemed harsh...unwelcome after the shadowed intimacy they had shared on the veranda. Winnie bent, efficiently loading the dishwasher. He knew Mrs. Cross wouldn't blink an eye if they left the sink piled with dirty plates and glasses. But already, he also knew that Winnie possessed the kind of caring heart that would show consideration to anyone, regardless of social station or bank balance.

He leaned against the counter until she finished puttering. When she finally faced him, he held out a hand. "Care for a walk? That was a lot of calories."

Seconds stretched into a minute or more. Winnie's face was troubled. "I don't know what happened last night," she said slowly. "But I'm not in the habit of sleeping with men I just met. Even if the Wolff name does carry certain reassurances."

"A walk, Winnie. That's all."

His promise coaxed a small smile. "I suppose it couldn't hurt."

"You want some shoes?"

She shook her head. "I love to feel the grass between my toes. I spent more money on the yard last year than I did on the house."

"Then I'll join you." Her eyes widened as he kicked off his shoes and stripped off his socks. But she didn't comment.

As they left the house via the main entrance, he deliberately steered her in the direction of the front gate. Most of his manpower was clustered around the two houses. So for some privacy, Larkin knew this was their best bet. They walked beside the stream, hearing little plops and splashes as frogs jumped into the water.

The grass was like velvet beneath their feet, cushy and

smooth. Larkin synced his pace with hers comfortably. He was playing with fire. A smart man would say good-night as he had the night before. In his life, he walked alone. Without apology. He needed the personal space, the isolation. So there was no place for Winnie. But memories of an abandoned kiss taunted him, bringing his erection to life with an ache that made him want to pull her down into the soft grass and lift her skirt to her waist.

The image and the urge were so strong, he had to drag air into his lungs in a great gulp.

Winnie didn't seem to notice his agitation. She hummed snatches of songs as they walked, her husky alto slightly off-key. It struck him with dark humor that their innocent stroll was as circumspect as if they were Elizabeth and her Mr. Darcy. Once, when Annalise was fourteen and desperately ill with the flu, she had made Larkin sit with her and watch that wretched movie twice through.

It was the only thing that distracted her from her misery, so Larkin had consented. Even Devlyn had lingered one afternoon to watch it with them. The two brothers had kept careful vigil as their beautiful sister grew to adulthood. Now she was married and had a baby of her own. The knowledge gave Larkin an ache in his chest.

Life never stayed the same. His family was moving on without him. But he didn't want what they had. He didn't want to ever face that pain again. The regret over failing a loved one. The Wolffs were mating for life…one by one. But not him. Never him.

Six

As they neared the end of the quarter-mile driveway, Winnie stepped away from him. He felt the loss keenly. Something about her comforted the turmoil inside him. Calmed him. Gave him a sense of peace.

She linked her hands behind her back and looked up at the stars. "This is why I don't live in the city," she said. "I love the space, the sky, the solitude."

"Do you like being alone?"

She whirled to face him, her face a pale oval. "What does that mean?"

"Maybe you use your dedication to your charges as a way to hide out from real life."

Tension arced between them. His accusation was perhaps unpardonable, though he stood by it.

"You have no right," she said, the words ragged, her hands fisted at her sides.

He grabbed her wrist, feeling the frantic race of her pulse. "Did I hit a nerve?"

"I won't discuss this with you." She yanked free of his hold.

His hunger and frustration rode him hard. To hell with what was smart. He had to know what she was thinking… what she was feeling. The uncertainty was eating at him, winnowing away the foundations of all his good intentions. "Did you kiss me because you're so damned lonely, or was it something more?" He took her upper arms in his hands and shook her gently. "Tell me the truth." Where was a moon when you needed one? He wanted to see her eyes.

Winnie stood motionless in his grasp, her rapid breathing the only evidence that she was upset. Gentling his hold, he ran his hands up and down her arms from shoulder to wrist and back. "Answer me, Winnie."

She stepped backward a second time, deliberately out of reach. "I'm alone because I choose to be." The words were barely audible. "I kissed you because you're gorgeous and appealing. That's all."

"That's enough." The sizzle of exultation eradicated his pique. He told himself to stay silent, but the words tumbled out. "I could say the same thing about you, Winnie. You exude a radiant sexuality that I'm fairly certain you don't even realize."

She ignored his comment, but he heard her breath catch. "It would be foolish for us to start something," she whispered. "Especially since we'll soon be surrounded by your entire family."

Her voice shook, sending a frisson of guilt along his nerve endings. He really was a selfish bastard. And his high-and-mighty personal code was no more than empty words. He was a man like any other man, driven by his need for a woman. Blind to reason, crazed by her delicate scent, he pushed for what he wanted, ignoring the yawning chasm at his feet that could lead to his doom. "Maybe we're not *starting* anything. Perhaps we're two loners enjoying the moment."

"And you don't see anything wrong with that?" He heard more curiosity than anger in her voice.

"Not at all. I think you're the most fascinating woman I've

met in a long time. I want you badly, even though I know it's a dangerous idea. I'm admitting my inconsistencies and trying to tell myself I can take advantage of a serendipitous situation as well as the next guy." He closed the distance she had created in two quick steps. "But if you're unsure, let's experiment. Maybe last night was a fluke."

She struggled briefly as he dragged her close, but moments later, she sighed deeply and leaned into him, raising her lips for his kiss. The quiet vulnerability of her pose gave him pause. Did he have the right to dally with Winnie knowing it wouldn't last? He knew he was rationalizing…telling himself he wasn't really straying from his personal code if this was nothing permanent. Even aroused to the point of pain, he saw the flaws in his reasoning.

But, hell…his brain was no longer in control….

He touched her lips with his…softly…reverently. The night sounds faded, leaving an expectant hush in their wake. Winnie's moan lodged in his gut. It took everything he had to keep the kiss gentle. He felt anything but gentle, and the ferocity of his need startled him. Winnowing his fingers into her hair, he palmed the back of her head and drew her closer, his mouth taking hers forcefully.

Her tongue played with his as one of her hands roved over his back. When they broke for air, she put her hand on his cheek. "It wasn't a fluke."

Just as he brushed the hair from her face, a bright flash of light startled them. It took only a split second to realize what was happening. Larkin bounded over the gate in hot pursuit of the photographer who'd had the gall to record a very private moment.

But the man had a head start, and he had an accomplice just down the road. As Larkin pulled up short, he heard the roar of an engine and saw the speeding vehicle disappear into the night.

Winnie was waiting for him on the road when he walked back. "Did you get a license number?"

He shook his head. "Too dark. Damn, I'm sorry. He must have been careful not to touch the fence, or the alarms would have gone off. And standing where he was, he wasn't breaking any laws."

"Don't feel bad. This has been going on for weeks. Now you know why I want to get away. It's only a matter of time until someone figures out that I'm hiding two dozen refugees. I thought you had guards everywhere. Why didn't your people come running when I opened the gate to follow you?"

"I have a remote in my pocket. I hit the *all clear* to protect your privacy. I didn't think you would want anyone to know we were out here together."

"Well, that ship has sailed, hasn't it." Resignation mixed with humor in her wry statement.

"Will this show up in the papers tomorrow?"

"Yes. And online. And anywhere else where that slimeball can garner a buck."

"My back was toward him. I doubt I'll be recognizable."

"Doesn't really matter. They'll make up a story anyway."

He gathered her into his arms and hugged her. "I'm sorry. I don't think I fully understood the scrutiny you've been under. My family has been hounded by the press over the years. I do know what it feels like to be violated."

She wriggled free, leaving him to wonder why. "It was bad when your mother and aunt died, wasn't it? I read about it in an old article when I was trying to decide whether to hire you."

"It was horrendous. I was young. I don't remember all of it. My cousin Gareth was the only one old enough to read the press accounts. I think it messed him up for a long time. But then he found his wife, Gracie. She's been able to bring back his ability to smile...to be happy."

"You all are a close family...I can tell."

"We've had to be. We weren't allowed to go to school until

college. So for all those years we had no one to play with, to study with, to squabble with but our siblings and cousins."

"Does it bother you that they've brought outsiders into your inner circle—all these marriages, I mean?"

He thought about it for a long moment. He and Winnie were walking slowly, side by side, retracing their steps to the house. *Was* he jealous? Did he feel a sense of betrayal? Perhaps he did. And it wasn't a rational thing at all. Winnie had picked up on an emotion he hadn't even admitted to himself. Was that why he clung so tightly to the notion that he didn't want to be needed?

"I suppose I do feel *something,*" he muttered. "But I'd like to think it's nostalgia for the past when we were a band of six and not something as petty as jealousy. I'm happy for all of them. I really am. But this tidal wave of marital bliss has happened pretty quickly. Kind of makes my head spin."

"It isn't contagious. You don't have to worry."

There was no mistaking the miffed tone in her voice.

"I never said I was."

She opened the front door and faced him in the foyer. "I don't need you to save me from myself, Larkin Wolff. If we end up in bed together it will be for a moment's pleasure. I like my freedom as much as you like yours."

He took her chin in his hand, running his thumb over her bottom lip. It was pink and puffy from his earlier kiss. The ache in his chest almost overwhelmed his good sense. "I'm selfish and stubborn and inflexible. I'd be a bad bargain for anyone."

Winnie stared at him, those amazing cat eyes unblinking. "Good thing I'm not in the market for a husband. Good night, Mr. Wolff."

By the time she had reached the third stair, he knew he wanted to stop her. But his stubborn adherence to a life mantra held him back—that and a healthy sense of self-preservation. His attraction to Winnie threatened to rewrite his personal code of behavior. Since meeting her, he'd bent more rules than he ever had before. Business. Pleasure. Never the twain shall meet. He inhaled sharply, ignoring his inclination to throw caution to the wind. "You'll need to pack tomorrow. And I'll finalize every last bit of the security plan. We can go over it together in the afternoon, and if all is well, we'll hit the road first thing Thursday morning."

Winnie paused and looked over her shoulder. "You're sure about this Wolff Mountain thing?"

"I am."

She nodded once. "Good night, then."

He watched her intently, seeing her slim legs and bare feet disappear from view. What would his relatives back home make of Winifred Bellamy? She was comfortable with money. So the Wolff riches would mean nothing to her. But she lived her life alone. And Larkin's family members were a boisterous lot.

He checked in with the night crew and then took a shower. His erection bobbed thick and full, giving lie to any notion that he wanted to take things slow with Winnie. He wanted her in his bed. Now. Or in hers. Hell, the location didn't matter. But he was going crazy wondering how long it would be before he could take her. And despite his mental gymnastics, it was definitely "when" and not "if." A man could lie to himself for only so long. Not even Winnie could deny that the connection between them was real.

The next day, it rained. The sullen weather suited Winnie's mood. She had made a mess of the covers last night, tossing and turning, unable to sleep. Part of her unease was apprehension about going to Wolff Mountain. But the encounter with the photographer had reminded her of all the reasons she needed to leave.

Midmorning, she worked in the dining room with her case files spread out and a half dozen lists in the making. She had hired a trusted friend to come and live in the house…to play Winnie's role as mother hen while she was gone. Larkin's team would keep intruders out, but there was much to be done with the day-to-day running of the estate.

When Larkin interrupted her just before eleven, she told herself she was irritated. But her pulse raced and her heart leaped in her chest. "Did you need something?" Her voice was deliberately cool.

He lounged in the doorway, so darned masculine and appealing he made a woman want to throw caution to the wind.

Larkin nodded. "I'd like to meet with the women as soon as possible. With you gone, I think it would be good for them to know how they'll be protected. Exactly who's on-site when, and how the security system works."

He had a good point. "How about right after lunch. I'll go down and explain why you're going to talk to them. Then I can call you to come."

"Works for me." He motioned toward the tabletop covered in papers. "You've never really explained how all this works. Is there a set time a family can stay? How do they 'graduate,' so to speak?"

She tidied a pile of folders and wished she could pretend he was just a man. Larkin Wolff did something to her guts. Call it pheromones or a crush or whatever…but in his presence she was jumpy and not at all herself. "It's different from case to case. When convictions are made and a husband or boyfriend is safely behind bars, the women can sometimes go home."

"And if not?"

"We have many women who will never press charges. Their only hope is to disappear. We have contacts who can help handle that. But it means moving to a new city, using a new name. No friends, no family. It breaks my heart." She heard the wobble in her own voice and took a deep breath. The only way she was able to help the women who came to her was to keep an emotional distance, though that was easier said than done. But like a doctor tending terminal patients, if she allowed herself to get too close, she would burn out rapidly.

Larkin stared at her in such a way that she felt exposed. She could almost see the wheels in his brain turning. "It must be very difficult to watch them leave," he said quietly.

Her throat burned with unshed tears. "I'd keep them all forever if I could. But then I'd never be able to take anyone new."

"And the problem never goes away."

"No. It doesn't."

He was wearing a blue knit shirt that matched his eyes. Though he appeared relaxed, she always got the impression he was like a panther ready to pounce at any moment.

"Winnie?" He straightened and shoved his hands in his pockets.

"Yes?"

"Someday…when you feel you can trust me…I'd like to know why these women mean so much to you."

Reminders of the past always brought nausea. Humiliation. "Can't I simply be doing my civic duty?"

"It's personal. I see it in your eyes. I'd be honored if you would share that story with me. When you're ready."

The kindness and compassion in his steady gaze threatened to turn her into a blubbering mess. "I need to make a phone call," she said, brushing past him abruptly before she succumbed to the tears his probing had caused. "I'll be down for lunch at noon."

Seven

Winnie never came down to eat. According to Mrs. Cross, Winnie was tied up on a conference call and having lunch at her desk. Larkin accepted the excuse at face value and took his Reuben sandwich out to the porch to eat. He loved Winnie's house. And he could only imagine how the peace and tranquillity helped heal the broken women who'd been given a raw deal.

As he stared across the lawn to the brick house in the distance, he tried to solve the puzzle of Winnie's past. She had declared her parents to be lovely people, even though they had no clue about raising a child. And he also knew Winnie had never been married. His background check had confirmed that. He hadn't told Winnie he had dug into her past. But it was part of the job. Trying to determine if an old disgruntled boyfriend might have read the article and seen a chance to grab the golden ring. But Winnie's past was an open book. At least as far as he had been able to discern.

She found him at one o'clock on the dot. Not giving him time to respond, she opened the screen door and headed out.

"I'm going now to tell them you're coming. And I'll explain why I feel it necessary to leave for a few weeks. I'll call you in about fifteen minutes."

Whatever Winnie had said about him must have quieted any fears over having a man in the house. By the time he arrived, the residents had gathered in the family room. Though the ragtag mix of women and children was unusually solemn and guarded in posture, their eyes were wary, not scared.

He introduced himself briefly, and then in layman's terms explained the various security measures he had installed. "You have nothing at all to worry about. I hire the best employees in the nation. They are discreet and committed to the job. But if you ever feel threatened in any way, this alarm by the front door will summon someone in under a minute."

There were only two questions. After that the women melted away, wraithlike in their ability to blend into the woodwork.

Esteban lingered, one chubby thumb stuck in his mouth. He removed it slowly. "We played outside today. *Mi mama* said it's because you put up that tent thing."

Larkin grinned. "It's called a tarp. And I'm glad you like it. How old are you?"

"Six and a half."

Larkin was shocked. The boy was small for his age, perhaps because of poor nutrition. "Do you like to read?"

Esteban shrugged in an oddly adult manner. "Don't know how."

Winnie whispered in his ear. "When they move around so much, it's difficult to get continuity in schooling."

Larkin felt a kinship with the boy despite the enormous disparity in their social situations. But one thing was different. Esteban had a mom and no dad. Larkin was just the opposite. He grinned at the boy. "I've got some baseball equipment in my truck. You want to see if your mom will let you hit a few in the yard?"

The kid's entire face lit up with excitement. "*Si!* I will go ask her."

He bounded out of the room, and Larkin glanced at Winnie. "Sorry. Guess I should have asked you first."

"No harm done. It will be entirely up to his mom. As you can imagine, the mothers tend to be very protective."

Esteban must have worded his request exactly right, because he was back in no time. "Let's go," he said, grabbing Larkin's arm. "I can hit a home run for you—*si?*"

Larkin retrieved his gear and took note of the fact that Winnie sat down on a park bench beneath a weeping willow to watch them. Esteban was a natural athlete. With a little coaching about batting and catching, he was soon snagging shallow fly balls and whacking soft line drives toward their audience of one.

There were undoubtedly people in the house watching, as well, but they kept themselves hidden. After an hour, Larkin called a halt. "I've got work to do, son. And you've done enough for one day. Don't want you to be too sore tomorrow."

Esteban beamed. "I'm gonna play for *los* Yankees one day. Will you come watch me, Miss Winnie?"

"Of course I will."

Larkin loaded the bats, gloves and balls he kept in the trunk for weekend games with some of the guys in his neighborhood back in his truck. Moments later when he turned back toward the bench, Winnie had disappeared. She was avoiding him. Perhaps for many reasons. He understood her reticence…but he didn't like it.

He strolled to the back of the property for one last pow-wow with his team. Every piece of equipment was working as it should. Winnie's beautiful estate had been encased in a bubble of security so tight, the First Family could come to visit without incident.

By the time Larkin hit the shower in his room to clean up for dinner, he was itchy and restless to see Winnie again. Even now he wondered if she would torpedo his plan at the last minute. His fears multiplied when he saw the note on the dresser.

> *Dear Larkin,*
> *I have several phone calls to make tonight, so I'm having dinner in my room. And I'll probably go to bed early. I'm sorry I won't be available for you to show me all the bells and whistles you've installed, but I trust that you've seen to every last detail.*
> *Winnie*

No *I'll see you in the morning.* No reference at all to their imminent departure. He felt his temper rise. Winnie knew she had to leave the premises. And if she thought he'd let her go to some anonymous apartment in a far-off city, she was deluding herself. Surely she wasn't going to refuse to go to Wolff Mountain. But she hadn't mentioned it either way.

He'd come up with a plan, and she had agreed to it. Nothing and no one would dissuade him from taking Winifred Bellamy to Wolff Mountain for her own good. Even if such an action was counter to his usual M.O. Now that the trip was hours away, his personal discomfort grew. The course he had set out was laden with pitfalls, no question. But it was too late. He'd have to live with the consequences.

He wanted Winnie. Only time would tell if he could resist temptation.

Winnie was awake at six, despite the fact that she had barely slept. She had half expected Larkin to pound on her door last night, demanding she come downstairs. It wasn't clear to her confused hormones if she was relieved or disappointed that she'd neither seen nor heard from him.

This morning, the dawning of the new day infused her with a restless sense of anticipation. She was deeply grateful to Larkin for everything he had done to make her property safe.

Today, she would be able to leave without worry. They still hadn't settled the matter of payment. The blank check was safely locked away in a drawer. Larkin refused to take it, and Winnie didn't know how much the job actually cost. That was a bridge they would cross later.

For now, all she had to do was determine how much and what to pack for an extended visit to Wolff Mountain. With all her new purchases—including some naughty lingerie that said louder than words what she was thinking—surely she had covered every eventuality. But she ransacked her closet just in case. In the end, she managed to get it all into two large suitcases, one garment bag and a smaller toiletry case.

Because she had avoided Larkin for the last half of the day before, she had no idea what time he planned to leave. Which meant that she had to face him sooner or later. She had dreamed about him last night. Hot, erotic dreams that were totally unlike her.

Larkin drew out a side of her she had thought long buried. It was disconcerting. And either thrilling or terrifying, she wasn't sure which. When she was dressed, she tiptoed downstairs for coffee. It was still only seven and Mrs. Cross wouldn't arrive for another hour and a half.

But when she opened the kitchen door, the smell of java wafted to her nose. She looked at Larkin, leaning against the counter, drink in hand. "I owe you one," she said lightly. She poured herself a cup and lifted it to her lips, inhaling the aroma with an inward sigh.

Larkin was heavy-eyed and unshaven, as though he had tumbled out of bed and headed straight downstairs. "Can you be ready to leave in an hour?"

The question was terse and perhaps a tad cranky.

"Yes." She took a long swallow, set down the cup and counted to ten. When that didn't work, she snapped at him. "What's your problem?"

He dropped his thick earthenware mug into the sink with

a clatter and turned to face her, arms folded across his chest. The short sleeves of the Leland Security polo shirt he wore fit nicely over muscular biceps. It was hard for her to remember that Larkin was as financially comfortable as she was, maybe more so. Nothing about him indicated that he had grown up as the offspring of an extremely wealthy father. Or that his family's interests spanned much of the globe.

Larkin gave the impression of being a self-made man, an entrepreneur who worked hard for a living. In a way, all those things were true. But add in the millions he stood to inherit and what was probably a very healthy stock portfolio thanks to Wolff Enterprises and Leland Security, and the picture shifted.

Larkin Wolff was a very rich man.

Which meant that if he was kissing her, it wasn't for her money.

His scowl and the dark stubble on his chin made him look dangerous. A man not to cross. He glared at her. "How long do you think you can avoid me? Or pretend that I haven't kissed you. Twice."

She lifted her chin. "I haven't been avoiding you," she lied. "There's a lot of preparation involved in my being gone for several weeks. I'm sorry if you feel I haven't been a suitable hostess."

Blue lightning flashed from his eyes. "You can take your damned etiquette and shove it. You *know* what I'm talking about."

"Wow. Someone woke up in a bad mood."

"God help me, Winnie. You'd better back off. I've had three hours of sleep and you're treading on thin ice."

"Back off or what?"

She took a step in his direction. Was she actually *trying* to make him lose his temper? She knew what anger could do to a man. It turned normally rational human beings into animals. Could Larkin be like all the rest? Would he explode?

His entire body seemed to tremble with fury. Unfolding his

arms, he closed the gap, thrusting his face close to hers. "You don't want to mess with me this morning. I'm warning you." His coffee-scented breath was warm on her face.

Fear mixed with an insatiable need to know. "Do your worst, big guy. I'm not afraid of you. Are you going to hit me?"

In an instant, his entire demeanor changed. His expression went blank, he backed off physically and a look of revulsion crossed his face. "Why in the hell would you ask me that?"

Now she felt ridiculous. And ashamed. As if she had hurt him somehow. "It's a fair question. You were furious." She didn't know what he was now. The entire mood of the room had changed.

Larkin scrubbed his hands over his face and leaned backward to bang his head softly against the upper cabinets. "I may be certifiably insane by the time you leave Wolff Mountain."

"What does that mean?" She was a calm, even-keeled kind of woman. No one had ever accused her of being temperamental. "If you weren't going to hit me, then what *was* going to happen? I saw your face. You were at the end of your rope. Aggravation times a thousand."

The flicker of a smile curved his lips. "Are you really that clueless about men? I've had a hard-on for the better part of twenty-four hours. You've been deliberately avoiding me as if I've somehow sullied your pristine reputation. It's called sexual frustration, Winnie. And *this* is what I was going to do."

He took her wrist and reeled her in, steadying her in the V of his legs while he took his time with her mouth. His agitation had apparently melted away, replaced instead with sheer male determination. Though he was gentle as falling snow, he overwhelmed her, surrounded her, mastered her. His coaxing kiss took the starch out of her knees and made her stomach quiver with helpless desire.

Standing became difficult, but Larkin held her shoulders in big hands, literally supporting her while he took what he wanted.

Suddenly, he pulled back, searching her face. "Put your arms around my neck, Winnie."

The gruff command was one she was happy to answer. She nestled closer to his broad, hard chest, and when their hips pressed together, she felt the strength and size of his arousal. Her compliance tore something in his control. Now his kiss was ravenous, stealing her breath, nipping her soft lips, tongue thrusting and mating with hers.

She shivered, lost to reason, ready to open herself to whatever he wanted. Because at this precise moment in time, she knew that she and Larkin were of one accord. Though she loved playing with the soft hair on the back of his head, she wanted more. Putting the tiniest amount of distance between them, she slid her hands under his T-shirt. His skin was hot, so hot. When her fingernail raked his flat nipple, he groaned.

The rush of power she felt at seeing him so vulnerable dwindled away to nothing when Larkin's hands shimmied up her thighs, lifting her champagne silk skirt. Breath caught in her throat. She should stop him. Any minute now. But not when he was making her feel so good she wanted to sob with the exquisite pleasure of it. He toyed with the elastic waistband of her underwear.

It was all she could do not to beg him to hurry. Long fingers delved beneath lace. Then he was touching her…intimately. At the spot where her body was soft and wet and aching for him. He probed gently, making her gasp and bury her face in his collarbone.

She heard his soft chuckle, but she knew, even then, that he was laughing not at her, but at both of them. At this incredible madness that had bloomed from nowhere. He stroked her rhythmically, building the intensity of her need. She wanted to tell him to stop, but she couldn't. Bliss lingered just offstage, a fiery release that frightened her.

Larkin kissed her ear, traced the curve of it with his tongue while he kept up his determined torture. Suddenly, he pressed two fingers into her aching emptiness. She cried out and sank her teeth into his shoulder as her body arched into his hand and she climaxed hard.

Seconds passed, perhaps minutes. Who knew? Her brain was fogged by afterglow. Even embarrassment couldn't intrude at that moment.

Larkin's voice rumbled in her ear. "You're amazing, Winifred Bellamy. Hot as a firecracker and so damned sexy you make my brain mush and another part of me hard as a steel spike."

"No one else has ever thought I was sexy." The truth spilled from her mouth uncensored.

He toyed with her swollen sex, sending little aftershocks throughout her body. "Then you've been hanging around with the wrong kind of men."

That sobered her. She wriggled away from him and straightened her clothing. The thin open-weave sweater that matched the color of her skirt was suddenly far too hot. "Not the wrong kind of men," she clarified carefully. "Just no men at all."

His poleaxed expression made her wince. "You're a vir—"

"Not technically," she rushed to reassure him. "But you're going to be disappointed if you think I know the *Kama Sutra* or really anything about how to please you. I don't. I can't. I should have said something sooner, but this whatever it is between us caught me off guard. Really, it's better if we stop this now."

"I should agree with you. I'm breaking rules right and left when it comes to you being a client." The dark look had returned to his face. "You make me question things I thought were carved in stone." He took her hand and placed it over his erection that throbbed, unmistakably hard and thick, through his cotton sleep pants. "But *this* is because of you, sweetheart. So I guess I'm saying to hell with my high-and-mighty principles. And I assure you, I'm not going to walk away just because you're inexperienced. I'll admit…I've never been with a woman who didn't know the ropes. But I guess that makes us even. Everything between you and me will be new territory."

"There is no *us*," Winnie said, feeling desperation clog her throat at his deliberate incomprehension. "You have to forget this idea. We're only going to be on Wolff Mountain together two or three nights. You said so yourself. It would be unbearable if we started something and it blew up in our face."

"Starting something with you is all I can think about."

Oh, God. Her cheeks flamed. "Don't you see? Even talking about sex is foreign to me. You're gorgeous and charming and I'm sure you have a little black book with names under every letter of the alphabet. I can't compete with that. Please forget we ever kissed."

"I can't." He said it simply, but with emphasis. "The kind of sexual tension and arousal that sparks every time we're in the same room together isn't some random occurrence. It's real. And powerful. I need to walk away. But I can't. At least not yet. You're stuck with me this weekend, Winnie. 'Cause you're to blame for the mess I've made of my famous *rules for living*. Sooner or later, you're going to be beneath me on soft sheets screaming my name when I make love to you until we both pass out."

She stared at him openmouthed. The picture he painted made her yearn for something she would never have, even if she gave in and agreed to be his lover. When the two of them became intimate…and she was ruefully aware that the timing was probably *when* and not *if*…Larkin would become her whole world. Even if she told herself she could be Bad Winnie and fool around with him just for kicks, the truth was, she would probably fall in love and he would break her heart. Because as he had made perfectly clear on more than one occasion, he was not a marrying man.

She wanted someone who loved her desperately. Many of the women in her care lied to themselves repeatedly, telling themselves that their men could change. If Winnie let herself believe in a future with Larkin, she would be making the same foolish mistake.

It was one thing to decide to enjoy a momentary liaison. And maybe she would if she had the courage. But to expect anything more would be akin to asking the moon to warm her like the sun. Larkin, though he might take her to the stars with his lovemaking, was no warmer than the moon. He was wonderful to look at, but like that silvery orb in the midnight sky, remote and impossible to reach when it came to true intimacy.

"I think we'll have to agree to disagree," she said primly, trying to ignore the butterflies in her stomach.

Eight

Larkin had never been in such a position. Only Winnie's inexperience kept the situation from being worse. He was a wreck. Sheer determination kept him upright, but he was perilously close to seducing her despite her objections.

Hot arousal pounded through his veins. His sex was swollen, and Winnie had no clue how desperate he really was. That fact alone was enough to make him put on the brakes in consternation. How could this quirky, artless female reduce him to such a state?

Larkin Wolff was one cool customer when it came to women. He never let his lust lead him down the garden path. Sex was great. And he wanted it. Often. But not enough to let any woman convince him he needed to be housebroken. Commitment to a woman meant personal responsibility, and he'd had enough of that to last a lifetime. Devlyn and Annalise were happy. Despite the fact that he had failed them repeatedly. Only his mother's untimely death had saved them all. So how could he contemplate making the sweet, generous, heartbreakingly vulnerable Winnie part of his life?

She wasn't the kind of woman to settle for meaningless sex. And if he couldn't promise her forever, what else did he have to offer? It was possible, given Winnie's physical reactions, that she might be okay with temporary if he gave her time to get used to the idea. He had promised to take her to bed. In spite of his better judgment, he was not going to be able to resist doing just that.

He studied her broodingly as he poured himself another cup of coffee and tried to pretend that she hadn't just rocked his world. She was dressed to play the part of an heiress today. Expensive but understated clothing…her long untamed locks forced into a socially acceptable style.

He far preferred the crazy hair, denim overall shorts and bare feet. That Winnie made him behave. This sultry, amped-up Winnie made him sweat. Both of them made him crazy.

The sound of the front door opening indicated Mrs. Cross's arrival. Winnie's wide-eyed panic might have amused him if he hadn't resented the interruption. "Come on," he said. He tugged her arm until she followed him out the far door of the kitchen and into the little corridor that led to the back staircase. Pulling his coconspirator with him, he moved quickly up to the second floor.

They stopped in front of his door. "I want you," he muttered, ready to drag her inside and show her how a man persuaded a woman.

Winnie's perfectly oval face with its high forehead and freckled cheekbones paled to the color of skim milk. "You'll get over it."

"Damn it, girl. Why do you have to be so stubborn?" He rested his forehead against hers, hands gripping her narrow shoulders.

"Think this through," she begged. She petted him with both hands as if he were a cranky toddler. "It's too quick, too ridiculous. I wish I could blame it on the full moon, but I'm confident that in no time at all you'll see we're doing the right thing by resisting whatever it is. I'm meeting your family this weekend…attending a birthday party. No matter how I respond to you or you to me, we shouldn't let this go any further. We can't be skulking around having naughty tête-à-têtes."

He swallowed his irritation and held her close, soothing himself with her presence, even as he felt the ache in his loins remain fierce and rampant. Maybe she was right. But he wasn't convinced. And he was no longer thinking clearly. "I'm not making any promises," he said.

She broke free of his loose hold and took three steps toward her room, hands clasped at her breast like a Victorian heroine who had narrowly escaped being ravished. "It's like the flu," she said. "You have to tough it out. I'm not irresistible, I promise."

He saw in her face that she was speaking the unvarnished truth. Or at least the truth as she knew it. Her lack of confidence in her femininity troubled him. When it came to her life's work, she was assertive…bold. And he had no doubt that she would fight to the death for the emotionally and physically damaged women and children in her protection.

But why could she not see how much he desired her, how beautiful she was, how special?

He cleared his throat, surprised to find it clogged with emotion. "What time is it?" He hadn't put on his watch earlier, hadn't even showered yet, for that matter.

"Eight forty-five."

"I told the pilot we'd be at the airport by ten-thirty. Can we still make it?"

"The pilot?"

"I asked my father to send the Wolff jet to pick us up. It's quicker and more pleasant than flying commercially, and frankly, I don't think I can be closed up in a car with you right now for several hours. Not when there's a good chance I'd pull off the road and have sex with you in the backseat."

"You're exaggerating," she said, her voice faint.

"I sure as hell am not. You don't know how close you came to having me take you standing up. That would have shocked poor old Mrs. Cross, now wouldn't it?"

"No one really does that, do they? Except in the movies?"

Her painful naïveté found a cynical spot deep inside him and softened it, made him want to smile despite his physical distress. "Meet me downstairs in twenty minutes," he said quietly, actually looking forward to this trip home. "I'll have the driver come up for your bags."

Winnie shifted her weight from one leg to the other. And she was barefoot. Again. "I mean it," she said, her pointed chin aimed at him in a stubborn tilt.

"Mean what?"

"You wouldn't enjoy it."

"Whatever helps you sleep at night," he said, taunting her gently, but realizing ruefully that she had him twisted in knots. "I've got plans for you, Winnie. So be forewarned." Perhaps he was warning himself, as well, because the consequences of deviating from his personal code were impossible to anticipate and likely to bring chaos and turmoil.

Even so, he had to have her.

Winnie brushed her teeth and threw her last-minute personal items into her bag. Her hands shook so badly that she dropped and broke a vial of expensive French perfume.

The fragrance was exotic, alluring…everything she was not. It was a gift last Christmas from her contact at the social services agency. Winnie had thought to take it with her to Wolff Mountain. Now it was ruined. Avoiding the glass, she touched her fingertips in the pale liquid and dabbed behind her ears and between her breasts.

The bit that remained in the bottle she put in a drawer. Perhaps it wouldn't evaporate before she got back. The air around her was heavy with the evocative scent. Suddenly, she flashed to an image of Larkin taking her here in the bathroom, their bodies slick with sweat. *Dear Lord.*

On shaky legs she walked back into the bedroom and retrieved her purse. She needed to say goodbye to Mrs. Cross and see if she had any last-minute questions. Leaving her door open so Larkin would know it was okay to get her bags, she walked downstairs.

He came through the front door just as she reached the foyer. His eyes widened when he saw her shoes. She had purchased a pair of taupe "big-girl" pumps with three-inch heels. The added height made her feel reckless. Larkin's eyes glazed over as he ran his gaze from her feet, up her legs, to her breasts.

Hot color flooded her face and neck. "I'll be in the kitchen," she said, turning away from him so she could breathe.

"The driver's here."

"I won't be long."

"What about your sub?"

"My friend will arrive in a little while, but we don't need to wait. She and Mrs. Cross have held down the fort for me before when I've had to be away." She fled just as the uniformed chauffeur entered, the man following Larkin upstairs for the luggage.

By the time she returned, Larkin stood impatiently at the front door. "Come on," he said. "We don't want to be late."

The limo was a deliberate choice. Larkin and Winnie wanted anyone watching to buy the story about Winnie heading to St. Barts. The driver had left the privacy window down. Larkin didn't ask for it to be raised. Consequently, conversation was minimal as they headed toward the airport just outside of Nashville.

It was just as well. Winnie couldn't think of a single conversational topic that would be innocuous enough to blot out the memory of what had transpired in the kitchen that morning. Larkin sprawled in his corner, his expression inscrutable, his gaze trained on the passing scenery. When it became painfully apparent that he was ignoring her, she checked messages on her phone, sent Mrs. Cross one last text about next week's grocery order and then mimicked Larkin's posture.

She had never flown on a private jet. When her parents were still living, the year she turned fourteen, they took her on one memorable family vacation...a ten-day tour of the Greek Isles. The airline tickets were first class, of course, but the flights, though very enjoyable, were nothing like the Wolff family jet.

The pilot greeted her pleasantly, and a single attendant seated her and offered beverages. Winnie felt like an interloper, especially when Larkin sat up front with the pilot and copilot. Eventually, she fell asleep.

When she awoke from her nap, they were circling to land at Charlottesville. Winnie had read that the Wolff property was tucked away on a mountaintop in the wilds of central Virginia. But she had no idea how long the trip from the airport would take. A second uniformed driver met the plane, transferred their luggage and offered box lunches he had picked up on the way.

Winnie was impressed. Larkin seemed to have every detail under control. After she finished her fancy sandwich, she dabbed her lips and glanced sideways at her companion. She had questions, a lot of them, but again, the presence of the driver kept her silent.

After an hour and forty-five minutes, when it was clear that their destination couldn't be too much farther, she finally broke her silence. "What will be expected of us tonight?"

Larkin drummed his fingers on the armrest. "Nothing more than a family dinner. Tomorrow I'll take you exploring. And we might be roped into decorating if it's not supposed to rain overnight. The party is Saturday at two."

"Outside?"

"Apparently so. My sister always was a risk-taker. The forecast calls for blue skies and upper seventies."

"She must be delighted."

"I'm sure it never occurred to Annalise that the outcome could be otherwise. She tends to charge full steam ahead."

"You love her."

His lips twisted in a faint smile. "I love all my family, but yes…Annalise is special. How she survived growing up in a house full of men, I'll never understand."

"And her husband?"

"Sam? He's been a family friend since we were kids. His father was the architect who designed Wolff Castle."

"Do you really call it that?"

He laughed. "We never intended to, but the locals began referring to it that way, and the name stuck."

Winnie kept the conversation going more for a distraction than anything else. As they reached the base of the mountain and waited for the massive gate to swing open, her nerves tightened. "So how did Sam and Annalise get together?"

"If you want to know what I think, I believe they've both had a thing for each other a long, long time. But they're both stubborn, Annalise even more than Sam. So it took getting snowed in during a blizzard for them to admit they had fallen in love."

"That is so romantic."

Larkin snorted. "Oh, it is. When they're not trying to kill each other."

"I thought you said they were in love."

"I did. But when you love a Wolff, life's not always easy."

Winnie looked out her window at the dense foliage, oddly disturbed by the tone in Larkin's voice. She wasn't in danger of falling in love with him, was she? Certainly not when he had made his feelings so plain.

Larkin was in lust with her. She was fairly certain his obsession would fade when they got amid his family. He would be too busy to pursue her. "When was the last time you were home?"

"Christmas, for a long visit. And a two-night stay right after my little nephew was born. I had to see him in the flesh to actually believe my rowdy sister could grow up to be a mom."

"She sounds like quite a woman."

"So are you." He stared at her, his gaze intent. "Outwardly, you and Annalise are nothing alike. But you both have a take-no-prisoners attitude when it comes to causes you care about. I think you'll like her."

After a winding journey that must have covered at least two miles, the car pulled up into a flagstone portico and stopped. It was markedly cooler on the mountaintop than down in the valley, and Winnie shivered briefly as the wind danced around them when they stepped out of the car.

The house where Larkin had grown up was monstrous in size and yet somehow appealing. It did indeed appear castle-like. Nestled in a clearing amid a forest of mixed hardwoods and evergreens, the behemoth of a structure looked as if it had been part of the mountain for centuries. But she knew the tragedy that drove the elder Wolff brothers to hide their children from society had occurred only a few decades ago. "C'mon," Larkin said. "I'll introduce you to the clan if anyone is around."

As it turned out, only the head housekeeper was there to greet them. Larkin's three cousins had houses of their own on the mountain, as did Annalise. And Devlyn and his wife, Gillian, weren't arriving from Atlanta for another couple of hours.

In the magnificent foyer, Winnie surveyed her surroundings with interest while the housekeeper pulled Larkin aside for a private word. Moments later the older woman led the way upstairs, leaving Larkin and Winnie to follow in her wake.

Winnie tugged on his hand, making him bend to hear her whisper. "What did she say to you?"

Larkin paused on a step, mischief lighting his eyes and taking years from his face. "She asked me if you would be sleeping in my bedroom."

Nine

It was all Larkin could do not to laugh out loud at Winnie's mortified expression. "Relax," he said quietly, sliding an arm around her waist. "I'm a grown man. She's just doing her job."

Winnie didn't look in the least reassured. "What did you tell her?"

For a moment, he thought about teasing. The temptation was almost irresistible. Especially when he imagined what it would be like if he and Winnie were actually lovers sharing a bed. The image made him hard. But Winnie was going to have a tough enough time assimilating into the large Wolff clan. No point in torturing her.

He sighed. "I said you were a good friend and that you would prefer your own room."

His answer appeared to mollify Winnie's misgivings, especially when the housekeeper stopped at the doorway of one of the larger guest suites. As the driver followed them in with luggage, Winnie's soft exclamation encompassed admiration and astonishment. "This is amazing," she said softly, walking forward to set her purse on the bed and turning in a circle. "I'll feel like a princess."

Larkin knew that Winifred Bellamy was accustomed to the finer things in life. But he had requested this room for his guest because it contained a touch of whimsy. And he wanted to spoil her. The enormous bed was covered in celadon-and-ivory brocade. Matching fabric hung from the canopy and flanked the large windows. Underfoot, sinfully soft carpet in a deep moss-green spread from wall to wall, broken up by a collection of feminine antiques that ran the gamut from chests to chairs to a chaise covered in ivory silk.

The housekeeper and driver had discreetly disappeared. "Well," Larkin said, "what do you think? I asked her to put you here. My quarters are just across the hall."

Ignoring him, Winnie flung open the French doors and stepped out onto the small stone balcony. Larkin couldn't have resisted following her if he had tried. The view of the surrounding forest intensified a feeling of complete privacy. Even birdsong ceased for a moment. The afternoon sun bathed them in gentle light.

He put his hands on her shoulders, feeling the warmth of her body, even through the thin fabric of her sweater. "I want you to be happy here," he murmured, nuzzling the back of her neck.

She stiffened. "Is all of this supposed to seduce me?"

The tart bite in her words nicked his pride. He turned her to face him. "I don't need help convincing a woman to share my bed. If you don't want me, all you have to do is say no." In the unforgiving light he couldn't find a single flaw. Her skin was luminous, her large, beautiful eyes mesmerizing. "Tell me *no* and I'll leave you alone."

They were so close he could feel the rise and fall of her chest as she breathed. "I never lie," she whispered. "Not even to myself. I do want you. But I fear we'll both regret it."

He took her hips in his hands, pulling her body flush to his, making her feel what she did to him. "I've thought the same thing. I can't give you the promises most women expect. But have you imagined pleasure for pleasure's sake? We're here now…alone. Why wait?" Though he hadn't planned it, he found himself kissing her. It was achingly sweet, particularly when her lips trembled and heated beneath his.

Slender arms encircled his neck. He felt her fingers sift through the hair at his nape. Something akin to an electric shock ricocheted through his body with a force that was as much pain as pleasure. The wanting overwhelmed him. Reason gave way to urgent passion and he lifted her and sat her on the stone railing. They were only on the second floor. He had her wrapped in his embrace. Safety wasn't an issue. But the eyes that looked up into his were clouded with apprehension. And that stopped him cold.

He rested his forehead on hers. "You're saying no, aren't you?"

"I want to say yes. But I can't. Not yet. It's too soon. I need time to understand this. One of us has to be reasonable." She played with his ears, an innocent caress that might as well have been her mouth on his flesh, so keenly did he feel the stimulation.

"What are you afraid of, Winifred Bellamy? God help me, I want to know." It was more than that. He *had* to know. And soon. Or he might lose his mind.

"I came here for a reason. To draw attention away from my home and to make sure the innocents in my care are safe. That's all."

"Let me make love to you," he muttered.

"Put me down, please."

He'd wanted to treat her like a princess, so surely he couldn't complain when she bossed him around. Lifting her in his arms, he carried her back into the bedroom and set her on her feet. "I know you want me," he said stubbornly. "You can't hide it."

She faced him bravely, her stylish shoes lending her extra

height. "Yes, I do. But mature rational adults know that some things we want are bad for us."

"Let me be the judge of that." He kissed her roughly, letting her feel the full force of his need. A hunger that made him a slave to her whims. Never had he felt so out of control with a woman, so unsure of the outcome. And suddenly, that knowledge enraged him. He'd spent most of his adult life creating an existence that was simple, easygoing.

Winnie had destroyed his peace of mind without even trying.

She was so damned unsure of herself. Not in life. She set goals and met them, doing work that few people would want to attempt. But when it came to her feminine appeal, her sexuality, she thought she would disappoint him.

The notion was ludicrous. Her vulnerability got under his skin and made him want to protect her in a very personal way. He should be running without looking back. But he was trapped by his own emotions.

He didn't need this. Not when in a very short time his entire family would have him under a microscope. Forcing himself to release her, he backed away. The expression on her face was as shattered as he felt. But it was her own fault.

"Dinner's at six-thirty," he said. "Can you find your way to the dining room?" He was being a horse's ass, and he didn't care. Sexual frustration did that to a man. He wanted to punish her for making him feel this way.

"But I—"

"But what, Winnie?"

She wrung her hands. "Maybe I should eat in my room. Your first meal at home should probably be just family."

"Oh, no," he said. "Your hiding up here won't accomplish a thing. And besides, I'm tired of being the only one without a date."

"You're a grown man. Surely you're capable of holding your own."

His mood lightened fractionally. "You'd think so, wouldn't you?" He decided his plan could backfire if he left her to her own devices. She might not show up. "Actually, why don't I stop by for you at 6:15?"

"What do I wear?"

"What you have on is fine…or something similar. It won't be so bad, Winnie. I promise."

"I still think it would have been less complicated for you to stash me in an anonymous hotel."

"But not nearly as much fun."

"If you flirt with me, they'll get the wrong idea," she pointed out.

"They've been decrying my single lifestyle for months. Maybe you can be my smoke screen."

"That's not a very nice thing to do to the people who love you."

"I'm not feeling very nice at the moment."

She had kicked off her heels and now stood in her bare feet, toes curling into the carpet. He'd never considered himself to have a foot fetish, but something about her small, narrow white feet seriously did it for him.

Winnie hopped up on the side of the bed, her legs dangling like a child. "What are you going to tell them about me?"

He shrugged. "That's your call."

"The truth is fine."

"Well, in that case, I'll just say you're a friend who's having some trouble. And that I wanted to show you Wolff Mountain. All of that is true."

She raised an eyebrow. "We're friends?"

"What would you call it?" He stared at her, not bothering to hide what he felt.

Her face went pink. "I'd be honored to be your friend. As long as you don't expect me to…" She trailed off.

"To share my bed?"

"Larkin!" She put her hands to her cheeks. "Quit saying

things like that. You told me you don't get involved with clients."

"That was before I met you."

"I'm boring."

He could see in her eyes that she believed it. She wasn't fishing for compliments, but he offered them anyway. "You're beautiful and sexy as hell. I could spend twenty-four hours in that bed with you and not be done."

"Is that even possible? I thought men…well…"

Her artless confusion amused him. "I might have to rest now and again, but you wouldn't be disappointed."

She wrapped her arms around her waist, rocking slightly. "I never said that was an issue. I'm trying to make you believe I'm not the kind of woman you're used to. And it would be embarrassing and awkward when you find out my shortcomings between the sheets."

This endless argument was getting them nowhere. He'd simply have to rely on proximity and the magic of Wolff Mountain to win her over. "We'll drop the subject for now. But it's not going away, I promise. Sooner or later, I'll convince you. So you might as well get used to the idea. Bringing you here was not one of my better ideas, yet here we are. I'm selfish enough to want to take advantage of the situation. Tell me you don't want me, and I'll leave you alone. But I don't think you can say that, can you?"

"Has anyone ever told you that you're arrogant?"

He grinned, looking forward to the days ahead. "I'm a Wolff. It comes with the territory."

Winnie fell back on the bed, her arms outstretched. What had she gotten herself into? Larkin Wolff was a charismatic, masculine man with enough macho hormones to put any female's heart in jeopardy. But she was a pragmatic woman. And she had discovered long ago that her life would be spent in the service of others.

The art of deep personal relationships was not something she had ever mastered. Even with her parents there had existed a distance created by devotion to their life's work and by Winnie's inability to express to them what she needed emotionally. In the aftermath of their deaths, she had lost her way for a time...with disastrous consequences. After that experience, she decided to pour her heart, time and money into something bigger than herself.

Knowing that she was protecting women and children who had few resources, either financially or otherwise, gave her a deep sense of satisfaction. The money in her various bank accounts had never meant much to her, other than the freedom to help those in need. Her personal fortune had complicated her life, and that same money was to blame for her misgivings when it came to Larkin.

For most of her life, she had been judged by the size of her financial bottom line. No one looked at Winifred Bellamy and saw a young woman with potential. All they cared about was what her net worth could do for them.

Larkin was different. He had no interest in her money. So why couldn't she believe him when he said he wanted her? She knew she carried scars—deep ones. But was she so damaged that the interest of a virile, appealing man threatened her somehow?

For the next hour and a half, she prowled the room, unable to sit down. The spacious apartment was peaceful and serene. Winnie's thoughts were anything but. She dreaded meeting the entire Wolff clan. Large groups made her nervous.

She doubted anyone would really believe the two of them were close friends. Larkin was the kind of man who went for sleek and sophisticated women. By his own admission, Winnie wasn't his type. She could hold her own in society settings. Her parents had included her in their entourage by the time she was ten years old. Charity events were old hat. Not that her mother or father had actually paid attention to her during the dinners and dances and auctions.

Winnie had always attended in the company of a nanny, seen but not heard. Nevertheless, she had learned what it meant to move gracefully through the world of movers and shakers.

Tonight's dinner, however, was different, more personal. And it was important to Larkin that his family believed he was happy. The thought made her laugh softly despite her inner turmoil. Surely they understood his renegade nature. His eyes betrayed his inner intensity.

Larkin was like a wild stallion masquerading as a civilized beast. When he touched her, she felt it. Whether tender or demanding, his intent was clear. He wanted to mate with her. But unlike his wolf namesake, not for life. Which meant she had to be on her guard until she knew her own mind.

She shivered as she undressed in preparation for a quick shower. Wrapping her hair in a towel, turbanlike, she caught a glimpse of her flushed cheeks in the mirror. Her pupils were dilated. Her breasts felt full and achy, the nipples painfully erect.

The outcome of this scenario was inevitable. She and Larkin would be lovers. Sooner rather than later. And it wouldn't be because of any coercion on his part. Her downfall would be the hunger that churned low in her belly, the writhing swirl of arousal that made her legs part restlessly and sent moisture to bloom in the folds of her sex.

Her entire body was on fire with longing. A deep, visceral need that had seemingly come from out of the blue. The life she lived had been pleasing to her, the days filled with purpose and activity. It was sobering to realize that meeting Larkin had exposed a gaping hole in her existence. She had friends, but no confidants. Acquaintances, but no one on which to bestow love.

The shower was quick. She could hardly bear to touch herself with soapy hands. In her imagination, it was Larkin bathing her, Larkin stroking her legs, her arms, her quivering belly.

By the time she made it back to the bedroom, her entire

body was trembling. If he saw her like this, he would know. And knowing would demand her submission to the erotic flame that danced between them.

Her throat raw with emotional tears, she drew back the covers on the bed and climbed in, wanting to pull them over her head. She had willingly walked into Wolff Castle. As a bolt-hole, the security was absolute. And it was a measure of her trust in Larkin that she had no fears at all about the charges she had left behind in Nashville.

But suddenly, and in blinding clarity, she realized that by coming with Larkin to his home turf, she had placed herself in tremendous danger. No one in her entire life had ever loved her enough to put her first. Even Larkin had been quick to point out that he wasn't interested in a conventional relationship that culminated in orange blossoms and wedding bells.

The truth seemed inescapable. She would go to his bed. How could she not? He was everything a woman could want in a man. Strong. Honorable. Virtually irresistible. He had revived in her a sexuality she'd thought long euthanized.

The resultant chaos in her soul was painful in the extreme, much like the awakening of a limb that had fallen asleep. She didn't *want* to want Larkin Wolff. She didn't want to *feel* anything for him. But she feared the damage was already done. With Larkin, she responded as a woman…whether she liked it or not.

Ten

She dozed off without meaning to, and when she jerked awake and glanced at the clock in a panic, she had just twenty-five minutes to prepare. Her hair was a challenge on the best of days. And of all times, this evening she wanted to appear chic and poised. A tall order for someone with her lack of height and a headful of frizzy curls.

She brushed out as many of the kinks as she could manage and then used a flatiron to tame the rest. With more luck than dexterity, she captured the unruly mass at the back of her head and secured it in a simple French twist. The diamond teardrop earrings she slipped into her earlobes were small enough for a family evening at home…given that the family in question was the Wolffs.

Standing in a recently purchased demi bra and panties, she surveyed the dresses she had brought with her. First impressions were important. And there were several ways she could go. Self-important heiress. Quiet outsider. Neutral onlooker.

Unfortunately, fashion was not always so easily labeled, so

in the end, she decided to go with *I-need-to-look-good-and-be-comfortable-'cause-I'm-gonna-be-on-display*. The dress she chose was red, but that was the only flashy thing about it. The fabric was a silk blend that felt sensuous against her skin. The sleeves ended just below the elbow. A narrow sash cinched her waist, and there was enough fullness in the skirt to swish nicely as she walked.

Although the back of the dress zipped to the top of her spine, the front dipped in what was for Winnie a daring V. She had always been embarrassed by her generous breasts. And it wasn't that they were abnormally large, but the rest of her was so small, they stood out. Her habit was to downplay them as much as possible.

Even now, the cleavage revealed was practically chaste. But as Winnie gazed at herself in the mirror critically, she could almost feel the heat of Larkin's gaze. The curves revealed by the dress would draw his eyes inevitably. Would he assume she had dressed to please him?

Tugging the bodice a bit higher, she sighed and went in search of shoes. Black patent-leather heels to be exact. She'd packed sling backs with pointed toes and stiletto heels. The shoes made a statement.

Her legs were as white as the rest of her, but she couldn't abide panty hose. And she didn't have the nerve to deck herself out in a garter belt and stockings. One hurdle at a time. Surely it was enough that she had bought new underwear. Which Larkin might or might not get to see.

With eight minutes left for makeup, she relaxed. Long ago she had given up trying to cover her freckles. Lip gloss and a dash of eye shadow were enough to transform her usual ultra-casual self into a fashionable, though lightly gilded lily.

When the knock sounded at her door, she sucked in a breath. Showtime. She flattened her hand on her stomach, seeking in vain to calm the riotous butterflies. Taking her time, she crossed the room and threw wide the door. "I'm ready," she said.

* * *

Larkin couldn't have been more surprised if she had greeted him stark naked. He swallowed hard, caught unawares by the sheer sexuality she exuded. He tried not to stare at her breasts. Never would he be so rude or gauche with another woman of his acquaintance.

With his throat dry and his jaw tight, he focused on a spot somewhere over her shoulder. "You look very nice," he said as he ushered her out into the hall and shut her door.

Winnie punched him lightly on the shoulder. "I believe that's called *damning with faint praise.* I was hoping for better."

He debated kissing her. Too damn risky. "Would you rather I told you you're so hot in that dress I want to take you up against the wall with my hands under your skirt squeezing your ass?"

His voice came out gruff, scratchy and hungry.

"Behave yourself," she muttered.

They walked side by side down the wide hallway, close, but not touching. His entire body was rigid. Though he loved his family dearly, he could consign them all to the devil at this exact moment. And if they saw the look on his face, they would be in no doubt about his plans for Winnie.

As they descended the stairs and headed toward the formal dining room, he concentrated on anything but the smell of Winnie's innocent scent. He didn't really care if his family speculated about the nature of his relationship to Winnie. But revealing his obsession was another matter entirely.

No one noticed them for several long seconds when they entered the room. Everyone was present and accounted for except the children. Larkin leaned his head toward Winnie. "The little ones are with a sitter tonight. Dad and Uncle Victor wanted a formal, grown-up dinner. It's rare that we all make it here at one time."

Suddenly, Larkin's uncle spotted them. Raising his voice and tapping his wineglass with a spoon, the old man boomed out a greeting. "It's about time you showed up. I'm starving."

Laughter broke out, and in moments Larkin was enveloped in a wild rush of hugs and kisses. He looked over his shoulder in the midst of the mayhem to see that Winnie had stepped to one side, a contemplative smile curving her lips. Their eyes met. He jerked his head, indicating his wish for her to join him. But Winnie waited until everyone melted away to take his or her seat.

Larkin remained standing and pulled her to his side. "It's good to be home," he said simply. "This is my friend Winnie Bellamy. She's been having some trouble with the press, so I'm stashing her here on the mountain for a couple of weeks until things blow over. I told her you all wouldn't mind. Do me a favor and don't overwhelm her. I'll give her the playlist while we eat, but take pity on her and remind her of your names if she forgets."

After a chorus of *Hello, Winnie,* Larkin held her chair, seated her and took his own place at the table. He realized almost immediately that all eyes were on him and his guest.

He sighed and muttered in a low voice. "I might as well introduce them all now. Or else we'll never get to eat."

Winnie nodded, looking a bit like the proverbial deer in the headlights, though he was pretty sure he was the only one who noticed. She had an innate sense of poise and composure that stood her well in the midst of this crazy group.

Before Larkin could begin, Victor Wolff stood and raised a glass. "I'd like to propose a toast."

Everyone lifted a wine goblet, including Winnie. Larkin listened, half wincing, to see what his outspoken uncle would say.

Victor was still bluff and dictatorial, but his manner had softened over the years. He and Larkin's father had been in their forties when they'd both married much younger wives. Now they were beginning to look like old men. "This family has seen its share of sorrow." He paused, his throat working visibly. "I never imagined that when you were all grown you would have the sense to pick such fine partners. I think I should have more than two grandchildren by now—" he slanted a stern look at Jacob "—but I am so damned proud of each and every one of you. To the Wolffs."

To the Wolffs. The toast echoed around the table, and Larkin felt his own throat tighten with emotion. It had been a long, sometimes dreary road, but now he finally had the satisfaction of seeing his brother and sister happy—really happy.

Larkin started to say something to Winnie, but Victor wasn't finished. "We're delighted Larkin brought along a friend. As cohost tonight, Winnie, I hope you'll allow me to present you to this somewhat motley crew."

Winnie nodded and smiled shyly. "I'd appreciate that, sir."

Victor put his hand on the shoulder of a large, fierce-looking man to his right. "This boy is my eldest, Gareth. Next to him his wife, Gracie, the only woman who has ever had the temerity to challenge our resident hermit." A titter of laughter circled the table, but Victor continued. "They have a precious toddler you'll meet tomorrow. Then we have my youngest son, Kieran, and his wife, Olivia. Kieran was our globe-trotter, but he's finally decided he likes a more permanent life here on the mountain, thank God. Their daughter, Cammie, is in grade school. And last but not least on my branch of the family tree is my middle boy, Jacob. I don't suppose you need an introduction to his spouse."

If Winnie was overwhelmed, she didn't show it. "Oh, no… not at all. Ms. Dane, I'm a huge fan."

Larkin's sister-in-law was an Academy Award–winning actress. But here at Wolff Mountain she was known simply as *Ariel.* Though she had been an official Wolff for some time now, she kept her stage name.

Larkin tensed momentarily, waiting for his father to stand. Vincent Wolff seemed far more frail than he had even a few months ago. But to Larkin's surprise, Victor continued his emcee duties.

"With my brother's permission I'll finish out the roster. His eldest is Devlyn sitting to his left, along with Gillian, who has been a part of this family one way or another for a long, long time. Devlyn runs Wolff Enterprises out of our headquarters in Atlanta. Beside Gillian is Sam Ely, again a longtime family friend. Sam had the guts to court our beautiful Annalise. They produced the newest member of the Wolff family just a few months ago. And I think that's it."

Annalise looked at her brother with a gimlet stare and then focused her pointed gaze on Winnie. "Winnie Bellamy? As in Winifred Bellamy, the heiress?"

Winnie felt like an animal at the zoo. Although the attention of Larkin's family was understandable, she felt exposed. Particularly when Annalise, whom Larkin loved dearly, asked what everyone else was thinking.

"That's me," Winnie said, wishing she had an ounce of Annalise's boundless confidence.

"And how did you two meet?"

"Annalise." The warning tone in Larkin's voice didn't deter his sister.

"Merely a commonplace question."

"It's okay," Winnie said, straightening her spine and tightly clasping her hands in her lap. "Larkin was doing some security work for me. He was kind enough to offer me a place to hide out. That's about it."

Beneath the table, she felt Larkin's big, warm left hand enclose her right one. He squeezed gently.

"Enough interrogation," he said. "I promised Winnie that you all were civilized for the most part. Don't prove me wrong."

His sister leaned over and kissed his cheek. "Whatever you say, big brother. We're all just thrilled you're here for a visit again so soon. Unprecedented, isn't it?"

Larkin's lips twitched in a small smile. "I had some vacation time coming."

"You can't even *spell* vacation," Annalise muttered.

The sibling banter halted when Victor rang a small bell, and moments later half a dozen servers entered the room. Winnie was granted a reprieve as the table sagged with an assortment of food that rivaled any elegant restaurant. She ate quietly, content to study the interplay between the siblings and cousins and in-laws.

The six younger generation Wolffs teased each other unmercifully, with the spouses interjecting occasionally. The affection and respect between Victor and his sons was unmistakable. A family bond that appeared to be unbreakable.

Larkin's father, however, was oddly withdrawn, and although he and his sons and daughter exchanged polite comments, to Winnie's critical eyes, it seemed as if there was some sort of odd, disturbing distance between father and children. Devlyn and Annalise and Larkin were tight—that much was clear. But something was different on that side of the table. Something intangible, but very real.

The long, drawn-out meal was enjoyable, but not exactly relaxing. Winnie was very conscious that she was under observation. Curiosity seemed a more likely impetus than any criticism, but she was still relieved when at nine o'clock the family began to scatter. Those with kids went to rescue babysitters. Devlyn headed upstairs to the office to discuss business with the two elder Wolffs. Gillian mentioned a phone call to her mother, who lived nearby, and Ariel was still suffering jet lag after returning home from a movie shoot in Australia, so she and Jacob said their good-nights, as well.

When the room emptied, Winnie glanced sideways at Larkin. They had both stood during the exodus. Now she shifted from one leg to the other, feeling the pinch of new shoes on feet that weren't accustomed to heels. In a matter of moments, given the size of the room, an unexpected sense of intimacy enclosed them.

Larkin's eyes danced. "Well, did you survive?"

She grimaced. "Your clan is delightful, but overwhelming. As an only child, I found myself envying you all that familial closeness. I know about the tragedy you all dealt with, but in an odd way, I have a feeling that your isolation growing up gave you bonds you might not have had otherwise."

"That's certainly true."

Something grim flickered in his eyes. Was it the memory of loss, or a more current pain? "Is your father okay?"

Had she not been watching so closely, she might have missed Larkin's tiny grimace. It was gone in less than a second, and his expression was closed when he shrugged. "Getting older. But yes."

"Do you get along? You and Devlyn and Annalise seem guarded when you talk to him." Larkin's features turned to stone and she knew she had overstepped her bounds. "I'm sorry. It's none of my business," she said hurriedly.

He stared at her for long seconds. "I'm not sure we've reached the point of exchanging confidences like that—have we?"

She knew immediately what he meant. Back in Tennessee when he'd pushed her to explain why she had opened her home to domestic refugees, she had balked. "Fair enough."

He brushed a thumb across her cheekbone, his touch sending little prickles of sensation down her spine. "I'm perfectly willing to answer your questions."

"But only if I reciprocate?"

He nodded. "You can trust me to keep your secrets, Winnie. We Wolffs are good at that…too good at times."

"I hardly know you."

"Doesn't feel that way." Larkin spoke the God's honest truth. His hand actually trembled as he touched her hair. Nothing diminished the ache he felt when he was close to her. Not even the presence of his loud, boisterous family. Beneath the thin fabric of her crimson dress her nipples beaded unmistakably.

He sucked in a sharp breath as his sex hardened. Pulling her close, he whispered in her ear. "I don't like it when you're quiet. I need to know what you're thinking."

"I'm thinking you know way too much about women." Her body leaned into his, trusting, fluid.

His chuckle was ragged. "I don't know the first damn thing about you, my dear virginal Winnie. Except the fact that you have a heart as big as Texas and you're stubborn."

"Pot…kettle. And I'm not a virgin."

"I may be stubborn—true—but I know innocence when I see it. I believe you. But there's far more to chastity than a technicality. Has any man ever gotten close to you?" He rested his chin on top of her head, wanting to take down her hair and run his fingers through it.

She shivered. He felt it. And his gut clenched. Someone had hurt this brave, delicate woman. Badly. He didn't know how he knew, but he did.

"I retract my question, Winnie. You'll tell me when you're ready. But for now, I need this."

She looked up at him, her green-gold eyes clouded with arousal. "This?"

"This." He lowered his head slowly, trying to rein in the thundering locomotive that was his libido. First he kissed her forehead, then her small, perfect nose. Skipping lush, moist lips, he tilted her head to one side and raked his teeth down her neck, nipping and licking until Winnie squirmed and panted.

"We're still in the dining room," she muttered. "Someone could walk in." The need to feel her hands on his bare skin drew a groan from deep inside him. Larkin was losing it. He could tell. And Winnie was right. This was not the place or the time. "Winnie," he croaked. "Are you willing to go to my bedroom? Now?"

She froze, her cheek against his shoulder. "I do want you, Larkin," she whispered. "More than you know. But I need to be sure. Sure that I won't regret this. You do something to me I don't even understand."

It was the catch in her voice, the bewildered dismay that brought him back from the edge. Winnie was strong and courageous and determined to handle whatever life threw in her way. But even so, she was so damned vulnerable, it broke his heart. He knew he had to protect her, even from himself.

He released her and stepped back, though doing so nearly bent him double with agony. More than anything in the world he wanted to bury his shaft inside her soft, warm body. He needed to see her face when she found pleasure. Craved the sensation of his body joined to hers.

"I won't seduce you into something you aren't comfortable with. But it might help to talk about it."

Eleven

For one long, pregnant moment, Larkin thought he had gotten through to her. But apparently Winnie was so accustomed to keeping her own counsel that it would take more than a promise of confidentiality to breach the walls she kept in place.

Her eyes downcast, she stood disconsolate where he had left her.

Sighing inwardly, he conceded momentary defeat. "Do you feel like going for a walk?"

Her head snapped up. "In the dark?"

"I know this mountain intimately. You won't get lost. But bring a jacket and put on some sturdy shoes. If you want to go with me."

Some of the strain left her face and she smiled. "I'd like that."

He dropped Winnie off at her room and returned fifteen minutes later to find her ready and waiting. Leaving the house was a last-ditch effort to keep himself from doing something he shouldn't.

The elegant woman with whom he'd shared dinner had disappeared, replaced by a more familiar, but no less appealing Winnie. She wore a shapeless sweatshirt, old jeans and low-topped hiking shoes. Her hair was still up in a twist, but it was looking a little worse for wear.

His mood improved drastically when she smiled. And as he ushered her in front of him down the stairs and out a side door, he felt a surge of excitement at the chance to share with her his childhood home. "I'll show you around the house tomorrow," he promised. "But for now, I want you to meet the mountain."

The night was black, the inky expanse peopled only by stars. With the canopy of large trees compounding the darkness, they were forced to walk slowly. He had a flashlight, but he knew Winnie would enjoy the experience more if they let their eyes adjust to the gloom.

He didn't hold her hand. Too much temptation there. But he supported her elbow in spots where the terrain was rough. Winnie had a long stride for a small woman, and he didn't have to slow his pace to accommodate her.

The silence between them was comfortable, broken only by the hoot of an owl or the rustling of unseen animals in the underbrush. The more he walked, the more the memories flooded back. He'd been very small when the family came here, perhaps not even five. But those early days were burned into his brain. He and Devlyn and Annalise had been shell-shocked over their mother's death.

And filled with a bone-deep relief that conversely tormented them with guilt.

"It's my turn," Winnie said, her voice muted to accommodate the night. "What are you thinking about?"

Larkin never talked about the past...not even with his brother and sister. They shared an unspoken but very real pact to try to forget the years that had damaged them. Perhaps the only way Winnie would ever come to trust him was if he told her the truth.

He just wasn't sure he was ready or able to go there. "I was thinking about what a beautiful night it is."

His blatantly false statement was met with silence. It *was* a beautiful night. But Winnie already knew him well enough to sense his disquiet. Cursing softly beneath his breath, he stopped and faced her. "Perhaps we should both keep our secrets. I've already told you I don't do permanent relationships. And if you and I are ships that pass in the night, maybe we should enjoy each other without all our baggage."

She looked up at him, but he couldn't make out her expression in the shadows. "That sounds very clinical and cold."

"Trust me, Winnie. I'm not cold," he said. Though his brain shouted *No!,* he kissed her. Her response was immediate, passionate. In his arms, she was perfection—sensual, sexy—as appealing and irresistible as a gulp of water to a thirsty man. The fire they generated continued to disconcert him, but he was prepared to ignore the little warning bells that clanged inside his skull. Because holding Winnie was rapidly becoming an addiction.

Even as her soft lips clung to his, he knew his timing was off. He couldn't take her on the cold, hard ground. Breathing jerkily, he held her at arm's length. Breaking the connection was an actual physical pain. He *had to* keep his hands to himself if he was going to respect her wishes and not push her into something she didn't really want. "C'mon. I have something to show you."

Winnie stumbled in his wake, her heart pounding and her legs weak. Already she craved his touch. When Larkin kissed her, she felt alive. As if the world was filled with delicious possibility. It was novel and delightful and scary as heck. What Larkin was offering was a purely physical, short-term interlude. And now he was willing to keep even that on a superficial level. Carnal pleasure…no emotional closeness. Her heart grieved even as her aching body told her that the outcome was inevitable. She wanted him to fall in love with her, to tell her he couldn't live without her. There was no one in her life she could call her own. No one to cling to in the difficult times. But Larkin was not going to be that man. So why was she even considering becoming his lover, when what she really needed was a man for the long haul?

She followed him for what seemed like miles, but was probably not all that far. The unfamiliarity of her surroundings and the depth of the night made everything seem strange and alien.

They had been walking a fairly level though rough trail. Now, suddenly, Larkin struck off up a hill, the path virtually invisible. But Larkin, like the wolves for which the family was named, was sure-footed and silent as he prowled. Winnie, not so much. She caught her toe on a root and cried out.

Larkin whirled around. "Are you hurt?"

"No. Not really. But I could use some help."

His patent reluctance to touch her might have made her laugh if the atmosphere hadn't been rife with sexual tension. His hand closed around hers, the palm large and slightly calloused. "We're almost there."

She gripped his fingers with hers and pressed close to his back. She wasn't at all sure what wildlife might be lurking just off course. Suddenly, they broke free of the tree line, and Larkin drew to a halt. His abrupt stop, combined with her momentum, propelled her into his back rather enthusiastically.

He drew her to his side. "Careful," he said.

At their feet, the world fell away into nothingness. Vertigo threatened for a few moments, but Winnie took a deep breath and reminded herself that Larkin would never let her come to harm.

The view in front of them was eternity, the valley below nothing but a dark void dotted here and there with pinpoints of light. Overhead, a concave bowl arced across the heavens, encompassing stars that appeared to reflect man-made illumination below.

Winnie gripped Larkin's hand, unaccountably nervous. "It makes my stomach jumpy," she whispered, not wanting to desecrate the hushed night.

He released her fingers and slid an arm around her waist. "You mean holding hands with me?"

Smiling in the darkness, she rested her head against his shoulder. "Sure," she said. "That's what I meant."

Kissing her hair, he pulled her in front of him and encircled her with his arms. "We loved to come here as kids. Devlyn even thought of trying to rappel off the side once, but thank God we talked him out of it."

"So you weren't a daredevil?" She loved the sensation of utter safety she felt in his embrace. For so long she had carried her burdens alone. The yearning to have someone with whom to share them was part of the reason she was unsure about making love to him. Larkin's presence in her life was limited. He would be a wonderful lover, she had no doubt. But without anything more, would the sex seem empty and meaningless?

She felt his laugh rumble against her back, his breath warm. "I could be wild on occasion. But for whatever reason, I was always the one trying to keep my big brother grounded and my little sister protected."

"Must have been exhausting."

"You have no idea. Now that they're both happily married, I feel free for the first time in my life. I've passed the torch to Gillian and Sam."

Though the tone of his voice was teasing, she knew she was hearing the unvarnished truth. And it explained a lot. Larkin didn't need any more complications in his life. His business was flourishing, but his personal life was a sailing ship becalmed on the sea. No waves. No danger.

And he liked it that way.

Though the night remained as impenetrable as ever, gradually Winnie began to see the light. Her life was not uncomplicated. She had chosen a path that would always involve a certain amount of personal sacrifice. And she couldn't imagine ever turning her back on the hundreds of women and children who sought refuge beneath her wing. If anything, she planned to build another house for boarders, another haven for the lost and hurting.

Such grandiose ideas didn't leave much time for relationships. And it wasn't fair to ask any man to sign on for a difficult journey not of his choosing. Larkin lived a life that had begun with unspeakable tragedy. But he had survived, thrived even, and had grown up to be an honorable man, a dutiful son and a caring brother. Certainly he deserved peace and happiness.

Winnie deserved those things, as well. She had allowed one egregious mistake in her youth to impact her life far more than it should. Like Larkin, she had survived certain challenges as a child, but she had become a decent, empathetic adult…at least she liked to think so.

Living like a nun was a choice she had made consciously. But now…in Larkin's presence, she understood what she had been missing. Her sexuality had been stunted, back-burnered. She still wasn't sure she had the erotic know-how to please a man like Larkin Wolff. But he wanted her here and now, and the opportunity to revel in a man's passion might not pass her way again.

Even if it did…the man wouldn't be Larkin. In the event that another handsome, charismatic guy crossed her path, she was pretty sure the temptation would not exist…not like now. Because Larkin touched something inside her. In a way no one ever had. He *wanted* her.

Her silence might have lasted ten minutes or thirty. In the midst of her soul-searching, Larkin had stood mute, a sentinel surrounding her with warmth and security.

"Thank you for bringing me here," she said softly. "It's impressive."

"Not beautiful?"

"More like awe-inspiring. As if I can see the whole universe and my place in it."

"Most people say views like this make them feel small or insignificant."

"Not me. I think this vantage point from your mountain reminds me that my little light shining down in that valley or up in that sky is important to someone. Somewhere. I make a difference. And that's important to me."

"Which makes what I told you about not wanting responsibility sound pretty shallow and selfish."

She rubbed his hand. "Not at all. You've built a company that helps people in important ways. And you're an integral part of a close, loving family. But you've chosen to protect your heart. There's nothing wrong with that. Especially in light of your history."

"I'm amazed that someone hasn't taken advantage of that Pollyanna attitude of yours. Do you ever see the bad in people?"

A knot formed in her chest, composed of searing regret and embarrassment. "Yes," she croaked. "Believe me, it happens."

Without warning, one of his hands slipped beneath her sweatshirt and slid up to capture a breast. When he jerked in surprise, she could tell he hadn't expected to find naked flesh. But then again, when she'd decided to leave off her bra, she hadn't anticipated fooling around in the forest.

She stood rigid in his embrace, jailed by two big arms encircling her and the chest of warm steel at her back. Larkin teased her nipple, sending a blast of heat from her chest to her belly. He weighed the fullness of her breast in his palm, caressing…lifting.

"God, you're so soft," he groaned.

As though he could decipher her incoherent thoughts, he moved back enough to bring a second hand into play, now holding her aching flesh in both hands, grinding his pelvis into her lower back. Her knees went weak, and she lost the ability to speak.

Now the sweatshirt was up to her armpits and Larkin had his fingers at the button of her jeans. She shivered as chilled night air danced across heated skin. Shaking her head in frustration at the impossible setting, she moaned.

Larkin bit the side of her neck, hard enough to leave a mark. "I want to make love to you, Winnie. Please. If you ask me to wait, I will, but it just might kill me."

He slid the flat of his hand down inside her pants, his fingertips brushing the lacy edge of her bikini panties. "Yes," she said, the yearning for him so thick and sweet, it threatened to choke her. "I want you, too…tonight."

Twelve

Larkin could barely process her words, so crippling was the haze of lust that engulfed him. Winnie was the kind of woman who needed to be courted…cherished. He was long past such niceties in this instant, and it took everything he had not to shove her down in the raw dirt and pound into her until the roaring in his head and the fire in his gut subsided.

"What did you say?" He was befuddled, torn by a knife-edged desire beyond anything he had ever known.

Winnie turned in his arms to face him, her bountiful breasts crushed up against him, her delicate fragrance driving him mad. She tilted her head backward. Even, white teeth gleamed as she smiled. "I said I want you, Larkin. I never really knew I could feel this way about anyone. My brain tells me this is a mistake, but I don't care. Take me to your bed. And show me how good it can be."

He was barely aware of the trip from the cliffs to the house. They moved rapidly, insanely perhaps, through the forest. He was terrified she would change her mind, and equally terrified that he was treading a path he would bitterly regret.

He was not only choosing to ignore his guidelines about mixing business and pleasure, he was rewriting the whole damn rule book. But the time for rational evaluation was long past. Even if this was a colossal mistake, he had to have her. Once inside the castle, he spirited Winnie up a remote staircase. In the dimly lit, seldom-used stairwell, he drew up short, his chest heaving. "Your room? Mine?"

Her tiny grin was adorably sheepish. "You gave me a suite for a princess. Let's live the fantasy."

He would have stood on his head and recited the Greek alphabet if she had asked him to. In fact, pretty much anything Winnie wanted was his new mission in life. At her door he glanced both ways to see if anyone was watching. The hallway remained empty, so he twisted the doorknob and ushered her inside.

He gulped hard. "Do you need anything?"

Winnie's eyes were huge. Her blush reached from her hairline to her throat. "I'd like to freshen up. I bought some new... well, in case..." She stuttered to a halt.

Larkin ground his teeth and managed to smile. "Fifteen minutes? I'll jump across the hall to my room and do the same."

Relief and shy pleasure beamed at him from those exotic eyes. "That would be great. You don't have to knock when you come back...just, well...you know...come on in." Now her cheeks were beet-red.

He backed toward the door, at some level worrying that if he lost eye contact with her, this amazingly perfect turn of events would go up in smoke. "I'll be back." It was more a vow than simple information.

She nodded, reaching into her suitcase and giving him a view of her heart-shaped ass. "I'll be waiting."

Larkin took a three-minute shower, brushed his teeth, changed into clean boxers and at the last minute added a knee-length navy silk robe his uncle had given him for Christmas. He'd left it here in his room at the castle, sure he would never wear it.

But something told him that if he walked back into Winnie's bedroom mostly naked, his lover-to-be might hyperventilate. The robe seemed a prudent choice. Not only that, but the pocket came in handy for a stash of condoms. He slipped across the hall and, as instructed, didn't knock…even though, technically, only twelve-and-a-half minutes had elapsed.

Winnie was true to her word. She was waiting for him. The room had been plunged into shadows. A single lamp burned on a low table near the window. She had pulled the hangings on three sides of the massive bed, leaving open only the ones facing the light.

Larkin had to walk around the edge of the bed to see her. The covers on the bed were shoved to the bottom of the mattress. Winnie sat cross-legged right in the middle, her hands clasped in her lap. Her lingerie was the product of good taste and unlimited funds. Likely French in design and construction, the aquamarine teddy trimmed in cream marabou left little to the imagination.

Cut high on the legs and low in front, the décolletage barely contained Winnie's lush assets. Her waist looked tiny, and the thin strip of fabric covering her secrets was not quite doing the job.

Her white skin glowed in the soft light, but her eyes were dark pools of uncertainty. He was glad of the robe now. Because it helped disguise the fact that his sex stood at attention, eager and ready.

He cleared his throat. "You look beautiful, Winnie. Kick-in-the-gut, drop-dead gorgeous."

Her teeth worried her bottom lip. "So do you." She gulped as her eyes slid from his mouth downward all the way to where his robe tented "Larkin…"

He shed his outer garment and boxers matter-of-factly and

put a knee on the bed, prepared to climb into the princess's hideaway.

She held up a hand. "Stop."

Dear God in heaven. He steadied his voice. "What, Winnie? What's wrong?"

Her chest rose and fell rapidly, her gaze locked on the erection he could no longer hide. He was certain she didn't realize what alluring things her distress did to her barely tethered bosom. "I'm scared, Larkin, that I won't know how to please you."

Relief made his head swim. "You let me worry about that, Winnie, my sweet." He scooted to where she sat and reclined on one hip, his head propped on his hand. Testing the waters, he used one finger to trace the curve where her naughty lingerie rode high on a firm, silky hip.

Winnie squirmed, her eyelids fluttering shut.

He laughed softly. "Don't hide from me, sweetheart. I want you to see us together. Flesh to flesh."

She opened one eye warily. "Aren't you going to turn out the light?"

"Oh, no, my little prude. I wouldn't miss this for the world." He grinned at her. "Take down your hair, Winnie."

"I don't want to. It's so messy when I do that."

"Please? For me?"

Her expression telegraphed reluctance, but when she began removing pins, the simple beauty of the act was unbearably erotic. She tossed the accessories on the floor and fluffed her hair with both hands. "Happy now?"

"Getting there," he muttered. He pulled her onto her back and laid his hand, open-palmed, on her stomach as he leaned over her. The slick, cool fabric was no barrier to his explorations. He stroked her everywhere, his heartbeat racing as she squirmed and panted.

When he touched her between the legs, she stiffened, and

her lashes closed tightly. "Relax, Winnie," he said. "I won't do anything you don't like."

One eye opened. "It has snaps." The soft, barely audible whisper communicated mortified interest in what he had planned next.

"I know." A wave of tenderness swamped him, tempering the hungry beast that rode him hard. He pressed gently at the groove between the pair of fasteners. Winnie groaned and lifted her hips.

He was rapidly reaching the point of no return. But there was one thing he had to know.

"Winnie?"

"Hmm?" She licked her lips.

"How many times have you done this? I'm not prying," he said hurriedly. "Your secrets are safe. But I need to know."

Long lashes lifted. Confusion warred with petulance. "One. Are you satisfied?"

"How long ago?" He'd had his suspicions, but hearing her say it aloud sobered him.

She flipped to her stomach, face buried in her arms. "Nine or ten years…give or take."

The litany of curses that trembled on his tongue clamored for release, but he didn't want to give her the wrong idea. Her innocence was a treasure to be unwrapped slowly. Though his impulse was to take and take and take, hearing the confirmation of her lack of experience told him that gentleness would be the order of the night.

Raw passion could wait. But at the very least, he owed her romance, courtship, tender seduction. He wanted to know why. Why him? Why now? But he had to be patient. Winnie would tell him eventually. He had to believe that. Or else he would go insane imagining the worst.

He tucked her hair behind her ear, exposing one pink cheek. "Thank you for telling me. I don't want to do anything to make you uncomfortable."

She rolled over, her chest heaving. Tears welled in her eyes but didn't fall. "I'm sorry I'm not more experienced."

"Good God, Winnie." He stared at her, aghast. "Why would you think it matters?"

"I thought you might be disappointed in me."

The way she said it made him think someone had told her such nonsense. And that she had carried it around all these years.

"You're perfect. Just the way you are." He shifted his body so that he was half on top of her. When he lowered his head for a kiss, he was happy to feel her arms come up trustingly to encircle his neck. She tasted like minty toothpaste and reckless temptation. Sliding his tongue between her teeth, he felt the moment when the tension in her body sagged and she responded to him.

She returned the caress with her tongue, but she was tentative, clearly shy. His pelvis rocked gently against her hip, letting her feel his need. The kiss lengthened, changed tempo. When he nipped her lower lip with sharp teeth, she cried out and curled a leg around his, moving urgently.

He changed positions, sliding down in the bed to spread her legs. Winnie's hands clenched the sheet, but she didn't protest. Putting his mouth over the two snaps, he wet the silk with his tongue. Winnie responded with a keening moan. He pushed harder, until the fabric nestled in her sex. Sliding a finger beneath the narrow strip of cloth, he found Winnie wet and ready, her body ripe with passion.

Concentrating on pleasing her, he ignored the demands of his sex. His erection was painful, throbbing eagerly. But nothing took precedence over Winnie. Not even his own body.

Slowly, teasing her with gentle touches, he released one snap at a time. Peeling back the lower part of the teddy, he blew softly on neatly trimmed blond curls. Winnie's back arched, her face damp with exertion. Watching her carefully to gauge her reaction, he slipped two fingers into her moist, swollen passage. Broken whimpers urged him on as he played her with shallow strokes.

The fit was snug, even around his fingers, and just thinking about what it was going to feel like when he took her the first time made him shiver with agonized anticipation. He used his thumb to apply delicate pressure to her clitoris. That was all it took. Winnie climaxed instantly, her body writhing as she sobbed out a choked version of his name.

After a moment, he returned to her side and gathered her into his arms, her face buried in his chest. He felt her thundering heartbeat, inhaled the warm fragrance of her damp skin. Her limbs were lax, her entire body limp and heavy.

Though he needed relief badly, he savored this interlude of peace. He had never felt such an undeniable urge to give and not receive. Pleasing Winnie might almost be enough to satisfy him, had it not been an eternity since he had lain with a woman.

He shook her gently. "How do you feel?"

She rolled to look at him, but he didn't release her. Her expression was half dazed, half bashful. "I feel incredible. You are amazingly talented at finding a woman's weaknesses."

"You bring out the best in me. And besides, it's not weakness—not at all. It's power. The utmost power of a woman over a man." He realized even as he said it that his words were true. Winnie possessed a certain level of control over him, and he hadn't understood the extent of that until just now. He was pretty sure he didn't like it.

She scrambled to sit up, scraping her wild hair from her face. "I want to make you feel good. Like you did me. But I'm worried you'll think I'm clumsy or foolish."

Again, those echoes of someone else's voice. He frowned. "Whatever you enjoy doing will make me feel good. Anything." He tucked his hands behind his head, hoping to convey that the next steps were hers.

She studied his face anxiously. "I want to do for you what

you did for me," she said. "But I'm embarrassed. Do you mind if I turn off the light?"

"I need to see you, Winnie."

"Please."

Reluctance gripped him, but he understood her reticence. Perhaps lack of visual cues would even the playing field. He had far more experience. But he had given her carte blanche. "Okay. But when you get up to turn off the lamp, I want you to undress for me."

He kept his voice even, unemotional. But her face paled before flaming with color. Her lashes dropped to shield her expression. "I will."

Though he tried his best not to let her see, his entire body was rigid with explosive lust. Tasting her, inhaling the scent of her arousal, had wound him to a fever pitch. And now his little Winnie wanted to play games. God help him. As she left the bed, he turned his head toward the light and saw her reach for the straps of her teddy. Since Larkin had already unfastened the garment between her legs, all Winnie had to do was lift it up and over her head.

She did so slowly, not looking at him. The innocent strip-tease beat anything he had ever seen advertised in Vegas. When she was completely nude, she froze, and he saw her inhale a deep gulp of air. Though she faced him bravely, she had yet to meet his eyes.

Her petite body was perfectly proportioned except for breasts that were on the curvaceous end of the spectrum. From his vantage point, he had not a single complaint. Raspberry nipples stood at attention. Her waist nipped in above hips that were the perfect anchor for a man's hands.

In the soft light, Winnie's skin was the color of cream. She reminded him of a famous nude he'd seen once in a museum. A vividly sensual, feminine beauty fixed for all time on canvas. Like her predecessor, Winnie's hair rioted around her narrow face. As he watched, she retrieved a hair band from the floor and brought the mass together in a messy ponytail.

When she lifted her arms, the shape and movement of her breasts made him weak. He wasn't at all sure he was prepared for what was to come. He'd had many occasions in his adult life to experience sexual arousal. What he felt at this moment and in this room was something else entirely.

At last Winnie looked at him, her arms hanging at her sides. He suspected that she wanted to cover the fluff of hair at the apex of her thighs, but she did not.

"Come to me, Winnie," he said, his voice hoarse.

She nodded jerkily, reached for the lamp switch and plunged the room into darkness. Moments later he felt the mattress dip when she climbed into their nest. Then he heard the rasp of rings on a metal rod as she pulled the final set of drapes shut, enclosing them in complete intimacy.

His eyes strained against the darkness. But it was as if he were blind. Only his imagination worked overtime, painting images of Winnie in his brain.

Her whisper broke the tension that held him. "Don't move your hands unless I say so. I can't concentrate when you're touching me."

"I'll try." He wondered if she realized what she was saying. Apparently he wasn't the only one subject to this madness.

When she first made contact, he wasn't expecting it. He flinched so hard that Winnie laughed softly. "Relax, Larkin. You can trust me."

The same words he'd said to her on more than one occasion. Had she phrased it that way with intent, or was she merely responding to his jumpiness? He inhaled sharply, unable to stifle a moan when her small hands gathered his balls and caressed them.

He worried that he might embarrass himself. She avoided his quivering shaft and ran her hands down his flanks, his calves. One at a time, she massaged his feet, pressing her fingers deeply into the arches, separating his toes and kissing them one by one.

Sweet Jesus. When had he become so damned susceptible to an innocent massage? He felt her test the tendon at the back of his heel, recognized the brush of her hair as it trailed across his ankle. He gripped his own wrists beneath his neck and held on, feeling like a prisoner drawn on a rack.

Finally, she abandoned his lower extremities and moved to the head of the bed. Leaning over him, she ran her hands from his shoulders to his waist. "You're so strong," she whispered. "I love that about you."

He sensed that her breasts swayed above his face. When she leaned forward an extra inch, he captured a nipple with his lips and teeth and sucked violently, dragging a cry from his temptress.

"The other one," he demanded, chivalry lost in guttural command.

Without protest she complied, her hands now braced on his pecs. Her flesh was firm and sweet, like the perfect summer peach. This time, he backed off, swirling his tongue around the areola with teasing, light touches. He wanted more, but he had made a promise, and he would keep it as long as he could.

Moments later she withdrew. The muscles in his shoulders ached. His erection had been tight and full for so long that the pain of arousal had muted to a burning fire that engulfed his entire lower body. He tried to regulate his breathing. Used an old relaxation technique from his college days when he'd been constantly horny and unable to sleep. Nothing worked.

The agony of his need for her surpassed his self-control. He was ready to cry uncle when, suddenly, he felt the brush of her lips on his sex and she took him in her mouth all the way to the root.

"Damn it, damn it…" He pumped wildly, his hands grabbing at her head, anchoring in her hair, as he exploded. His release went on and on for seconds, minutes, aeons. Winnie, instinctive in her innocence, sucked him gently, even as he came, turning him inside out and leaving him weak as a baby with her head lying on his chest.

"Turn on the light," he croaked.

She traced a fingernail on his flat belly. "No." She had yet to touch him with her hands. Not where he wanted it the most.

"This isn't up for debate. I want the lights on. Now."

Her fist closed around his limp shaft, shocking it to life with a million volts of power. He groaned, insanely out of control. "I'll do it myself." It was an empty threat.

The humor in her voice called his bluff. "No, you won't." Gently she learned the rhythm that hardened him, that made his aching flesh ready for more. He wanted to grab her and take what was his. But he had promised her the driver's seat, and some last thread of honor kept him docile beneath her torture.

Nothing she had done so far was out of the ordinary. Only her shy enthusiasm and his growing hunger for intimacy with her transformed the night into a fantasy. He was resigned now to being blind. Lord help him when he made love to her with the lights on. The sensory overload might turn him into a slobbering maniac.

Gradually, his shaft returned to full attention. His recent release had only taken the edge off his hunger. When Winnie ran her finger across the drop of fluid that signaled his readiness, he sensed her leaning back on her haunches. "Okay," she said, her voice breathless. "You can do it now."

"Do what?" In his current state, he couldn't decipher the riddle.

"You know…make love to me." Even in the dark he could detect her embarrassment at having to say it out loud.

He chuckled hoarsely, winded and panting. "Oh, no, baby. You've done everything right so far. Climb on top of me and take what you want."

Thirteen

Winnie barely recognized herself. Begging for darkness had been a stroke of genius on her part, because it had allowed her to explore without Larkin's knowing gaze tracking her every movement. But now he'd laid out the ultimate challenge.

She thought of the size of him and her long dry spell. A technical loss of virginity a decade ago hadn't prepared her for sexual acrobatics with Larkin Wolff. He was big and hungry and nowhere close to being satisfied if the thickness of his sex was any indication.

The silence lengthened. With the bed hangings pulled shut, the air had grown moist with their breathing, almost uncomfortably warm. But turning on the light was something she couldn't manage. Not yet. *Climb on top of me and take what you want.* Larkin's arrogant demand sparked her indignation. Did he really think she wouldn't have the guts?

"Where are the condoms?" she asked, proud of her steady voice.

"On the bedside table."

She reached out through the curtains, located one and laid it on his chest. "You take care of this. Then put your hands behind your head again."

He didn't respond verbally, but she heard the rustle of a packet and the sound of latex being rolled into place. Even in the dark, she blushed.

After a moment of silence, she knew he was ready. Gingerly, she slid a leg across his waist and wriggled until she sat on his chest.

Amazingly, Larkin remained still and compliant, though he wheezed. "You're a tiny thing, but I need to breathe, love."

His careless use of the four-letter word made her heart contract. He didn't mean anything by it. Just something a guy said to make a woman feel special. Well, heck...it worked.

In response to his plea, she scooted lower, now with Larkin's impressive equipment bumping up against her butt. The need to feel him inside her overrode the last of her inhibitions. Carefully, she lifted onto her knees, guided him with her hand and positioned the broad blunt head of his sex against her opening.

The vulnerability of the position gave her pause, but Larkin remained silent and unmoving, shoring up her confidence. Slowly, her breathing jumping all over the map, she forced herself downward, filling her emptiness with Larkin's life and power. There was some discomfort, but no actual pain. He was big and fully erect. Somehow, the fit was perfect.

She lay forward, finding his lips with hers and kissing him wildly. Without her noticing, he had released his hands and now sifted his fingers through her hair.

"Why are you crying, baby?" he asked, the words tender and soft.

"It's so wonderful. Why didn't I know how good it could be?" Her entire world had shifted on its axis, gravity no longer a certain force.

"Because you hadn't met me yet."

She slapped his cheek halfheartedly, wanting to deflate his

ego, but knowing he had good cause for his arrogance. "Feel free to take over anytime you want," she muttered. "I think I've exhausted my limited repertoire."

In truth, she didn't want to move. At this angle, she felt deliciously possessed, completely at his mercy with his muscular arms wrapped tightly around her waist.

Apparently she'd had no concept of how her "no touching" rule had constrained him. Scarcely had the words *take over* left her mouth before he had flipped them, placing her beneath him with her arms outstretched over her head and her wrists manacled in one of his big hands.

He nuzzled her nose with his. "You surprised the hell out of me, Winifred Bellamy. To hell with inexperience—you're a natural."

She caught her breath when he flexed his hips, driving himself even deeper. Any moment now, she expected him to move, to climax, to do *something*. Desire curled low in her belly, dancing along her nerve endings and demanding to be sated.

"Shouldn't you be getting started?" She lifted her butt off the bed a millimeter, trying to give him the idea. But Larkin was heavy. And not willing to be pushed.

He braced himself on one hand and toyed with her breasts, plucking and twisting the nipples until he forced a groan from deep in her chest. The sound of her own pleasure startled her. She was lost. Larkin wasn't hers to keep, but after tonight, how could she ever let him go?

Wrapping her legs around his thighs, she begged. "I can't bear it, Larkin. Do something. Say something. Please. I need you."

Perhaps he had been waiting for a sign. Or the white flag of surrender. Whatever the reason, he finally snapped. Withdrawing almost completely, he slammed into her, shaking the bed and shouting hoarsely as he repeated the rhythm again and again. Reality blurred. The lack of light was disorienting.

Only the connection forged by his determined thrusts kept her grounded.

Something frightening in intensity built at the spot where he entered her. She'd climaxed earlier, but this was different. That had been an ecstatic relief. This climb to orgasm was darker, more erotic, infinitely terrifying. Everything inside her clamored for more and more.

Larkin's skin was hot and damp against her breasts. His mighty legs parted hers inexorably, giving no quarter. She wanted to wait for him, wanted to feel the dual explosions of release. But her body betrayed her.

Fingernails digging into his back, she cried out and hung on as everything around her incinerated, flared to a white-hot heat and vaporized. Vaguely she heard Larkin's growling shout as he followed her. He rode the final wave endlessly, his body claiming hers again and again until her world went dark as exhaustion rolled over her.

Hours later, Larkin woke up. Even with the bed hangings closed, the faint light of dawn pecked in through cracks. He cataloged the current situation with bemusement. Winnie lay sprawled beside him, facedown, her cute little ass only half covered by the sheet. Larkin was hard. And he wanted her again. But he also didn't want Winnie to be embarrassed by someone discovering that they had slept together.

Later he would sneak away with her somewhere on the property and tell her what last night meant to him, but for now, he had to protect her privacy.

His hand hovered above her head, wanting to touch her hair. But it might wake her. Though it pained him both mentally and physically, he eased from the cozy nest they had created, found his boxers and stepped into them. With the robe in his hand, he opened the bedroom door an inch and peered into the hall. No sign of movement.

With a sigh of relief, he made it to his room undetected. It was the custom, when all the cousins were in residence, to take an early-morning hike together. Annalise was still nursing the baby, but the guys would be expecting him. Maybe if he walked hard enough and fast enough, he could ignore the giddy feeling in his chest that made him want to stay in bed all day. Winnie Bellamy was dangerous. What in God's name had he done? He had crossed his own line in the sand, but somehow he had to maintain a degree of separation. He needed some space to make sense of this.

Winnie was having the most wonderful dream. Larkin Wolff was making love to her. And his eyes were telling her she was the most beautiful, desirable woman in the world.

Then her alarm started beeping. Groaning at her own stupidity, she reached for her phone and realized she wasn't in her bedroom at home. It took her three swipes at the bed hangings to poke an arm out, locate her phone and silence the alarm she'd forgotten to turn off before she went to bed.

Only then did she fully realize where she was. Memories of the night came flooding back. Her head snapped around. The other side of the bed was empty. The pillow was still dented, but Larkin was gone.

Humiliation made her tremble, but she shoved back the negative emotion. There could be a million reasons Larkin hadn't lingered to say good morning.

Her hand over her mouth and her chest heaving with nausea, hateful words from the past echoed inside her head. *You're a naive fool, Winifred. No man will ever want you for the long haul. You're ridiculously clumsy in bed, you look like a scarecrow half the time and you haven't got an ounce of feminine allure. No one cares about you. Do yourself a favor. Find the nearest nunnery and sign up, 'cause you're a disaster as a woman.*

It wasn't true. She knew it wasn't true. At least not all of it. It had taken several expensive years of therapy and the clarity of hindsight and growing maturity, but eventually she had recovered from the physical and mental trauma of her first sexual experience. The mere fact that she wanted Larkin so desperately and had embarked on an affair with him proved that she had healed.

The scars, however, ran deep. She had buried herself in her causes and closed herself off from emotional engagement. Her money had always isolated her to some extent. And having a vicious, amoral man destroy her self-esteem had made her withdraw from the world. In the aftermath she'd had to rebuild herself from the ground up. At twenty-three she'd stumbled upon a dire need in the social services network, and she had known almost from the beginning that it would be her calling, her passion to help.

She had confidence in herself as a person of worth and as someone who could achieve any goal. But despite her progress in every other arena, she'd still been unable completely to shake the notion that she was an asexual being. A female, but not the kind of *woman* who could hold a man's interest.

Meeting Larkin Wolff had changed all that. In fact, what had happened in this room last night was pretty much a miracle. But the fact that he had left without waking her spoke volumes. She wasn't stupid. She had given him pleasure. For a man like Larkin, though, pleasure was readily available in an infinite number of beds.

Winnie was grateful to him for showing her that she had more to offer than she had realized. Now it would be up to her to keep things comfortable between them. One night of amazing sex was a gift to her, an experience she would never forget. Not in a million years, however, would she let him think she misunderstood what it meant.

They had come to Wolff Mountain to draw attention away from her home. And to let Larkin enjoy time with his extended family. Already, both of those purposes were being fulfilled.

She would not cry, but there was nothing she could do about

the ache in her chest that made breathing difficult. As she selected clothing for the day, she was infinitely glad she had forced herself to go shopping before leaving Nashville. The Wolffs were elegant, sophisticated people—at least what she had seen of them at dinner last night. Winnie needed the reassurance of knowing she looked her best.

The outfit she chose was one she particularly liked. Beige linen slacks with a thin, lilac cashmere sweater. The top was short-sleeved and V-necked. She added pearl studs and a platinum chain with a single pearl attached. Her breasts were a bit more noticeable than she liked, but in the mirror she saw a woman whose visage was serene and dignified.

It took only moments to brush out her hair, secure it high on the back of her head and French-braid the ponytail. Sliding her feet into low-heeled calfskin pumps, she went in search of breakfast.

Wolff Castle—and yes, she was going to refer to it that way in her head, because the appellation fit—was quiet as a tomb. Fortunately, she had a good sense of direction and was able to find her way back to the dining room. She didn't expect to be served there, but as she had suspected, one of the doorways connected to an amazing kitchen and a much smaller breakfast nook.

Annalise was in residence, reading the morning paper with one hand and juggling a small child on the opposite knee. She looked up when Winnie walked in. "Good morning, Ms. Bellamy."

"Call me Winnie…please." Winnie took the seat on the opposite side of the table, and in moments, a plump woman in a traditional gray dress and apron brought a carafe of steaming coffee.

Annalise waved a hand. "The coffee is South American. I'd mainline it if I could. Enjoy yourself."

The older woman took Winnie's request for eggs and toast and disappeared.

Annalise's quick visual assessment of Winnie was a bit disconcerting, though her expression was more curious than critical. Larkin's baby sister was an incredibly beautiful woman, with a fall of jet-black hair and dramatic cheekbones. Winnie knew Annalise had grown up in a house full of men, but with a baby in her lap, she was the epitome of a peaceful Madonna.

While Winnie drank her morning jolt of caffeine, Annalise filled the silence. "Larkin headed out early with the guys. The five of them love tramping across the mountain together. It doesn't happen all that often anymore. I usually go, as well, but I'm nursing and can't leave the baby that long."

"What is his name?"

"Sam and I battled over that, but in the end, we settled for Phoenix. I know it's pretentious, but our family rose from the ashes, so it fits."

"I've read about the tragedy, of course. I lost my mother, as well, but I was much older. It must have been unspeakable."

Annalise shrugged. "I was the youngest. I barely remember any of it. So I guess you could say I'm lucky."

At that moment, Sam Ely walked through the door. "I wondered where you'd gotten to." The tall, sleepy-eyed man with chestnut hair took the chair beside his wife.

She leaned in for a kiss. The casual domesticity of parents and child stabbed Winnie's heart.

Annalise passed the baby to her husband and buttered a muffin. "I thought the guys invited you along."

He yawned. "They did. But I had a conference call at six about the London project, and we just now finished."

"London?" Winnie had been there many times and knew the city well.

Annalise's face glowed with excitement. "We're going there for three months. I can't wait."

The server brought Winnie's breakfast and also handed Sam an enormous plate of food without asking. Apparently his preferences were well-known, because he dug into it without missing a beat.

His wife scowled. "It drives me nuts that he can eat like that and never gain a pound."

Sam grinned. "Gain all the weight you want, darlin'. There will just be more of you to love."

Annalise hooted with derision, but in her eyes Winnie saw the deep immutable knowledge that she was loved. Envy was not a pleasant emotion, but Winnie acknowledged it. Would she ever come close to having what Annalise possessed?

Quietly eating her meal, she wondered why Annalise and Sam were here at all, when their own house sat not far away on the mountaintop. Larkin had told her all about his cousins' homes. Only Devlyn and Larkin did not have permanent abodes on the mountain.

Annalise patted her lips with a napkin and leaned her elbows on the table, chin in hand. "I've never known my brother to bring a woman along for a family weekend. What's the deal?"

"Annalise…" The warning note in her husband's voice didn't faze her.

"Well, I want to know, damn it."

Sam glared at her as he covered the baby's ears.

Annalise grimaced, still looking at Winnie. "Sorry. I gave up cursing two years ago, but it hasn't stuck."

Winnie smiled, charmed by Larkin's assertive sister. "Well, I—"

"You don't have to answer that, Winnie." Sam held up a hand, still giving his wife the evil eye.

"It's okay. No big secret," Winnie said. "As Larkin told you, I've been having a bit of trouble with the press. He thought it would be a good idea for me to hide out here until things die down."

"It was that 'richest women in America' article, wasn't it?" Annalise scowled.

"Unfortunately, yes."

Sam wiped drool from his son's chin. "My wife is jealous she wasn't included. When we got married, she put the bulk of her fortune in a trust for our children. Making her a kept woman. I like to keep her barefoot and pregnant."

"You are such a pig." Annalise, laughing, threw a strawberry at him. Then she turned back to Winnie. "But the more important question—is there anything going on between you and my brother?"

Winnie froze. Being a bad liar was a handicap. "Well, I…"

Fourteen

"Leave her alone, brat." After walking for miles over and around Wolff Mountain with his brother and three cousins, Larkin had paused only long enough to strip out of his sweat-soaked clothes and take a shower, before going in search of Winnie. He wasn't pleased to find her being interrogated by his sister.

Annalise had a knack for intimidation. Though in truth, Winnie didn't seem upset or anxious. He had expected one of her shy smiles when he walked into the room. She did smile... but the expression in her eyes was guarded—certainly not the look of a woman who had spent the better part of the night wrapped in his arms.

Mindful that he and Winnie hadn't discussed whether to keep their intimacy a secret, he settled for brushing her shoulder with his hand as he sat down beside her. "Morning, Winnie. Did you sleep well?"

She nodded, and for once, there was no pretty pink blush to reveal her state of mind. "Very well, thank you. I've been enjoying breakfast with these three lovely people."

Sam snorted. "That's the polite version. Annalise has been badgering her."

"I most certainly have not." His wife glared at him. "But at least now I know why they're here."

"You told them?" Larkin shot a sideways glance at Winnie, surprised, to say the least.

The slight shake of her head gave him a warning. "I explained that the article has been causing me some headaches and that you convinced me I should lay low here for a while."

Ah. Not the whole story, but enough to appease his sister. As the maid entered the room, Larkin pointed at Sam's plate. "I'll have what he's having, please. I'm starving."

Winnie had finished her meal but was enjoying a coffee refill. "How far did you walk this morning?" Her tone indicated polite interest, nothing more.

His blood began to boil. It was one thing to hide the level of their relationship from his family, but another entirely to treat him like a virtual stranger. "I have no idea," he said evenly, as the maid came back into the room and placed his breakfast in front of him before exiting. "We run part of the trails, do some rock climbing, tramp through the overgrown woods. It's more of a ritual than a walk or a hike. Wolff Mountain has always been here for us. We like to remind ourselves of that whenever we come home."

"When *you* come home, you mean. The rest of us are here on a regular basis."

His sister was baiting him, a game they often played, but one that was not appreciated this morning. He wanted to get Winnie alone and see what the heck was going on.

He paused, fork in midair, and frowned at Annalise. "Devlyn doesn't."

"But Devlyn runs the company from Atlanta. He has an excuse. You don't."

Surprisingly, Winnie spoke up in his defense. "Larkin's firm is very well respected in Nashville. People I know speak highly of him. The business is not exactly something he can run from a distance."

Larkin felt his neck get hot. His sister was looking at him with barely veiled incredulity. Not only had he brought a woman over the threshold of Wolff Mountain, it appeared he was allowing that woman to fight his battles for him.

He cleared his throat and set down his fork. "Annalise is merely trying to needle me. It's what she does. The only reason *she* has a house here is because she married an architect, and he indulges her every whim. Most of the time they live outside of Charlottesville."

Winnie grinned. "I was an only child, so this sibling-rivalry thing is new to me. Carry on."

Sam stood with the baby. "I'm going to take this little bruiser back home and give him his bath. Stay and talk if you want to, honey."

Annalise rose, as well. "I won't stay where I'm not wanted." Grinning, she walked around the table and stood behind her brother, leaning down to give him a big hug. "Whatever the reason, I'm glad you're here, Larkin. I miss you. We all do."

The trio departed, and suddenly, the room fell silent. Larkin took another bite of his breakfast. Winnie's eyes were trained on her coffee cup. The two of them were surrounded by several doorways, any one of which might usher in the next intruder. It was not the place for a serious conversation.

Larkin shoved back from the table, leaning his chair on two legs. "How about I show you the house?" His plan was to get her alone and demand to know what the hell was going on.

She stood up. "Later perhaps. I need to call home and make sure everything is okay."

"I can save you some time." He reached in his pocket and handed her a slip of paper.

"What's this?"

He lowered his voice. "It's a live link to the site where my people post their reports four times a day. The female staff I've assigned to the safe house also include brief case updates on each of your women and children." He paused. "The password is *F-F-L-O-W*." When she looked blank, he chuckled. "That's *Wolff* spelled backward."

"Oh."

"I thought you'd like to keep up with things, so you wouldn't have to worry."

Still standing, she looked down at him. "This is very thoughtful of you. I appreciate it." Not one indication from her that they'd been naked together a few hours before.

"That's what you're paying me for." He got to his feet, pissed and ready to pick a fight. But Winnie didn't react to his sarcastic comment. What in the hell was going on inside that head of hers? Just when he thought he had her figured out, she disappeared into some place he couldn't reach.

He wanted to kiss her. Badly. He was pretty sure that physical contact could break through this weird impasse. But not with the possibility of an audience.

"Come let me show you around." He kept his tone coaxing, gentle.

She shook her head. "I'm really tired," she said. "I'd like to go to my room for a while."

"You just got up." He was losing it, and he could feel his frustration in the corded muscles of his neck and the way his breakfast churned in his stomach.

Winnie grimaced. "Your family is charming, but rather overwhelming. I'll be down for lunch, I promise."

Leaving him to stand there with his mouth hanging open in shock, Winnie walked out of the room.

She made it to her suite before the tears started in earnest. Making sure the bedroom door was firmly locked, she flung herself across the bed, buried her face in a pillow and sobbed. *That's what you're paying me for.* How could she have forgotten, even for a minute? Larkin Wolff was in her employ. He took care of things, because that was his job. Sleeping with her probably fell under the heading of fringe benefits.

The stress of the past month caught up with her. At least that was what she wanted to blame for this hollow feeling in her chest. Not since her parents died had she felt such a sense of loss. Which made no sense, because Larkin was not hers to lose. He was honorable and kind and sexy as hell, but he was a free agent. He'd told her so. And she had believed him. But last night in bed her world had been turned upside down. So much passion and tenderness surely came from a place of affection at least.

No rationalization made the situation any more palatable. But she had never believed in feeling sorry for herself, so after fifteen minutes of crying that made her eyes swollen and her cheeks blotchy, she forced herself to get up, wash her face and make a plan of action.

On the worst days of her life, she had always survived by creating a list, checking something off and telling herself that tomorrow would be better. If that was what she had to do in order to remain sane during her exile on Wolff Mountain, she would do it.

Still feeling shaky and sad, she got out her computer and used the link Larkin had provided. Seeing in print how well things were going back home lightened her mood significantly. She cared deeply about each woman and child who came through her gates. Little Esteban had really carved out a place in Winnie's heart, and it would be wrenching to see him go. But the whole purpose of what she did was to ensure that women could eventually make a new start in a home where they felt safe and happy.

The sound of a car engine outside her window enticed her to peer through the curtains and see what was going on. As she watched, Gareth and Larkin climbed into a Jeep and headed off down the drive. Conflicting emotions bounced around in her head. Relief that she didn't have to face him for a little bit. And sorrow that he was gone.

She spent some time unpacking her suitcases, and then decided to explore the house on her own. It was a deliberate attempt to sidestep any notion Larkin had of coaxing her into fooling around in some out-of-the-way corner of his castle.

The house was huge, but laid out in such a manner that it made sense. Starting in the charming attic, she made her way from floor to floor, memorizing the location of various rooms such as the library and the solarium. Doors of unoccupied rooms stood open, each one pristine and ready for guests.

She found Annalise's teenage bedroom still with posters of bands and fashion icons on the walls. None of the boys' rooms had been preserved in that way as far as she could tell. The few doors that were closed didn't tempt her in the least. She had no interest in snooping.

Once she made it back down to the ground floor she was ready to follow the smells of lunch being prepared, when suddenly, Vincent Wolff stepped out of what was unmistakably his office.

Once upon a time he must have been a handsome, impressive figure. Now he was stoop-shouldered, and his skin had a sallow tone that bespoke ill health. "Ms. Bellamy," he said. "What a nice surprise. Do you have a moment to chat?"

His tone indicated he wasn't really asking a question. Echoes of the dictatorial entrepreneur he had once been shone from fierce eyes.

Winnie grimaced inwardly. "Of course."

He seated her and closed the door. "Would you care for a drink?"

She shook her head. "No, thank you."

The old man poured himself a finger of whiskey and sat down in a leather chair opposite its twin, where Winnie perched. He knocked back the liquor, set the glass on a table at his elbow and studied her. "Larkin has never brought a woman here. You must be special."

"We're just friends."

Vincent Wolff's harrumph carried a world of disbelief. "When he was in his early twenties, I had to pay off at least three bimbos who were after his money. Sometimes young men think with their dicks."

Winnie's face flamed with embarrassment. She gripped her hands in her lap, speechless.

Vincent chuckled. "Good Lord. If my plain speaking makes you turn red as a tomato, I'll have to watch my words. I apologize."

"Thank you." Was that the correct response? Winnie felt the walls closing in on her.

Vincent picked up an empty pipe and chewed on the stem. "I know you've got more money than you'll ever need."

She swallowed. "That's true."

"So maybe you're actually in love with my boy."

"Larkin and I only recently met."

"Doesn't matter. His mother and I first set eyes on each other at Christmas and were wed by Valentine's."

Winnie was beginning to wish she had taken the drink he'd offered. How was she supposed to escape this inquisition? "Nevertheless," she said, her voice steady. "Larkin and I are not in a relationship."

"Are you sleeping with him?"

"Excuse me, but you just stepped over the line." Fury bubbled in her veins as she stood up and strode toward the door. He might be Larkin's father, but she would not sit here and participate in such an inappropriate discussion.

Her hand was on the doorknob when Vincent stopped her cold. "Larkin is a complicated man. You seem like a nice girl. But you should know that."

Winnie turned to face him, her face hot with a combination

of temper and distress. "If Larkin wants me to know certain things, he'll tell me."

"Forewarned is forearmed."

"I'm only here for a short visit. I know all I need to know about your son."

"I doubt he'll marry you."

Ice formed in Winnie's chest. Vincent wasn't trying to cause trouble. He seemed genuinely concerned.

She didn't respond. She couldn't. And her feet were glued to the floor.

Vincent stared into the empty fireplace, his gnarled hands gripping the chair arms. "The others think just because they're all happy as clams, that Larkin will follow suit. But they're wrong. He's got demons in him that keep him isolated from the pack. We rarely see him. So don't let him break your heart, Ms. Bellamy."

Winnie jerked open the door and ran. Lunch no longer had any appeal. She fled down the main hallway, and headed for the stairs that led up to her room. But before she made it to safety, Larkin came strolling around the corner.

He froze when they met, his eyes darting behind her, assessing, drawing conclusions. "Where have you been?" he asked, his voice harsh with suspicion.

She inhaled sharply, not accustomed to lying. "Your father asked me into his office so he could get to know me."

"I doubt that. The old guy likes causing problems."

"Well, he didn't."

"What did he tell you?"

"Nothing, Larkin. He was surprised you had brought me here, and I told him we were just friends."

"You can say that with a straight face after last night?"

"Last night we were curious and we scratched an itch." It was more for her—so much more. But that was irrelevant.

Larkin's jaw tightened and his eyes flashed. "Come with me."

Fifteen

Larkin took her wrist and pulled her into the nearby library. He closed the door and locked it for good measure. "What in the hell did he say to you?" His father had long ago given up the right to meddle in Larkin's affairs. And the old man had no business messing with Winnie's head.

She faced him, arms crossed over her chest. "What happened between you and me last night had nothing to do with your father. You were curious...so was I. About a spark we both felt. Now we've dealt with it."

He deliberately closed the distance between them and wanted to punch something when Winnie backed away. "Believe me, Winnie," he growled. "Last night only scratched the surface." Even arguing with her, he was so aroused, he could take her there on the desk.

Her jaw wobbled, and her eyes were damp. "I gave it my best shot. And you seemed to enjoy it. But that's all I've got. I'm not good at sex. I have no natural aptitude and no repertoire of fancy tricks to keep a man interested. Besides, I'll only be here for a little while and then we'll go on with our separate lives. The sex was meaningless."

He gaped at her, slack-jawed. "That speech has so many holes in it, I don't know where to start."

"Then don't. You know I'm right."

"I sure as hell do not." He was shouting, and he didn't mean to be. Winnie stood there in her rich-girl clothes looking pale and determined and painfully vulnerable.

He clenched his fists, lowering his voice to a more civilized level. "I don't know where you got the idea you weren't good at sex, but that's the stupidest thing I've ever heard you say. You don't have to know thirty-one positions and how to practice tantric sex in order to make me happy...hell, to make *any* man happy. You're smart and driven and incredibly generous. Not to mention that when you smile, my knees go weak."

"That's nice of you to say."

"I'm not being nice," he yelled. "I'm telling the truth. And the sex wasn't meaningless."

A knock sounded at the door. "Everything okay in there? Lunch is ready in ten." Devlyn's deep voice was unmistakable.

"All good," Larkin replied, clearing his throat. "See you in a minute."

Footsteps disappeared down the hall.

He stared at Winnie. "We're not done with this," he said, grinding his teeth at the knowledge that he couldn't get her alone for hours. Annalise had commandeered anyone without kids to decorate the tent she'd had set up out under the trees for tomorrow's birthday party.

Winnie shrugged. "You and I may have to agree to disagree. And why does it matter in the end? We're not a couple."

"People can enjoy a sexual relationship without signing a contract," Larkin insisted. "And if we enjoy being in bed together, that's important in and of its own right."

"Maybe for some men and women, but not you and me. We've muddied the waters. You're working for me. Now that we've done what we did, your family is bound to pick up on something. And to be quite honest, now that I'm here and I've met your cousins and siblings and their spouses, it seems kind of sleazy."

"We're lovers, Winnie." He dared her to dispute it.

"We *were* lovers," she corrected. "Once. Not anymore."

Sometimes words simply didn't do the trick. He took her by surprise, pulling her close and kissing her softly when all he wanted to do was strip her naked and slake his thirst. "Once will never be enough for me, Winnie. I got a taste of you last night…literally. And I can't stop thinking about it."

Winnie tried to shove him away, but it was a halfhearted protest at best. "I don't want to get attached to you, Larkin."

"Then don't. Use me as your boy toy."

His droll comment startled a laugh from her, and he felt some of the tension ease from her body. "You'll say anything to get what you want," she said with a sigh.

"It's one of my finer qualities." He slid a hand under her blouse. The fabric was crisp white cotton, hemmed neatly to hang over the waistband of a khaki skirt. Winnie's skin was soft and warm. He groaned, leaning his forehead against hers. "You have no idea what you do to me, do you?"

"You have a significant sex drive," she said primly. "I happen to be the nearest fish to your net."

"Not any fish will do, Winnie. And it makes me angry when you say that. You don't have a clue how appealing you are. I want to eat you up like ice cream on a hot summer day." He kissed her deeply, trying without words to communicate his need. Their tongues met, tangled. When Winnie struggled to get closer, he groaned.

Her fingers toyed with his belt buckle, making him wonder if he could make do with a five-minute quickie. But he shoved temptation away. He wanted to show her that she was special. He put a few inches between them, ostensibly to catch his breath, but in reality because he couldn't play this game and not take it to its inevitable conclusion.

Winnie sighed. "I'm confused, and I hate the way that makes me feel. Wolff Castle is wonderful, but I'd rather be at home in my own bed."

He peeled back the cup of her bra and stroked his thumb across her nipple. "You wound me, Winnie."

Her eyelids fluttered shut, her features etched tightly as desire gripped them both. It wouldn't take long to pleasure her, but perhaps at this juncture in time, it might be best to leave her as hungry and hurting as he was.

She whispered his name. *"Larkin."*

The yearning in those two syllables made the hair on his arms stand up. He wanted desperately to give in…to give up. But as surely as the sun crossed the sky, someone would be back to summon them to lunch.

"We have to go," he muttered.

"I know." The words were barely audible.

"Tonight we'll try my bed."

He waited for her to demur, to protest. But instead, she simply smiled at him wistfully and shook her head…which could mean anything or nothing.

He didn't have time to figure it out. This time it was Annalise who pounded on the door. "Come on, you two. Uncle Victor says we can't eat until everyone is at the table, and I'm ready to start gnawing on my napkin."

Larkin flung open the door, giving his sister a death stare. "Your manners leave something to be desired."

She pinched his cheek. "If you didn't want us mucking around in your business, you never should have come home."

He saw Winnie smile, but she didn't try to mediate the argument that was as familiar as it was sweet.

Fortunately for Larkin and Winnie, the lunch crowd was reduced. Gareth's family and Kieran's were eating at home, though they would be back in the evening.

Over hearty bowls of chili and homemade corn bread, Ariel, Jacob's wife, studied Winnie to the point of rudeness. Finally, her husband intervened. "Does she have food on her chin, or are you hoping to sketch a mug shot?"

Everyone laughed except Ariel. "I don't mean to offend," she said with a winsome smile. "But, Winnie, you have extraordinary bone structure. The camera would love you."

Winnie eyed her warily, perhaps a bit in awe. Even Larkin, who had known his cousin's wife for some time now, had to admit that Ariel Dane was exquisite.

"I'm not sure what you mean," Winnie said. "It's not false modesty to say that I'm definitely ordinary."

Ariel's smile encompassed everyone, but still her gaze lingered on Winnie. "It's your eyes, and the shape of your chin. Your perfect skin. Has anyone ever told you that you look like a young Meryl Streep?"

Larkin stepped in. "I thought it the first time I met her."

Winnie seemed more horrified than complimented. "You're being kind."

Ariel shook her head vehemently. "You don't see it, perhaps, when you look in the mirror. But your face is so expressive when you speak. And your voice—wow, all Southern and husky…"

Larkin decided he had to rescue Winnie before she died of embarrassment. "Back off, Ariel," he laughed. "Winnie is far too shy for Hollywood."

"But—"

Jacob put his hand over his wife's mouth. "I'm sure Winnie appreciates the compliment. Now…can we change the subject?"

Ariel grumbled good-naturedly, and soon the conversation shifted to less personal topics. Winnie lapsed into silence. Larkin leaned over and whispered in her ear. "If you're finished eating, let's blow this joint and go for another walk. This time you'll actually be able to see things."

"Sounds good to me," she said fervently, her expression

hunted. For a woman who lived alone, all this togetherness was probably a bit much.

Larkin made their excuses, and while Winnie changed clothes, he checked his email. Everything in Nashville was going well, but it was a good thing he was going to be back in the office come Monday. Work was piling up, and though his staff was top-notch, the boss was the boss for a reason. On the other hand, the thought of leaving Winnie on Wolff Mountain made his chest hurt. So he had a problem.

Using an anonymous tip line, he'd leaked info to a couple of the more outrageous tabloids that the heiress Winifred Bellamy was vacationing on St. Barts. His deliberate deception must have worked, because his man in charge of Winnie's case reported no sightings of paparazzi either in the air or on the ground.

When Winnie rejoined him, he grinned. "I like a woman who doesn't spend a lot of time primping." Winnie rolled her eyes at him and didn't comment. She had changed into neat navy shorts and a yellow tank top. And her sparkly white tennis shoes looked suspiciously new.

Larkin took her in a direction opposite the way they had walked the night before. "Kieran and Olivia have a house out in the woods."

Winnie balked. "I don't want to drop in unannounced."

"Don't worry. It's not them we're going to see."

Winnie followed him along a meandering path, enjoying the warm spring day and the peace and solitude. She was, by nature and experience, a person who was happy with quiet. It gave her time to think…to reflect. And with Larkin Wolff in her life, the opportunity to take stock of each day was important.

He was leading her into something they both wanted, but she was sure the consequences for her would be painful. This interlude had a definite end. Once Larkin was back on his home turf, Winnie would revert to being his client and nothing more.

She watched him as he walked in front of her, his stride easy, his broad shoulders straining the seams of a blue knit shirt that matched his eyes. Inexplicable as it was, she had no choice but to believe him when he said he wanted her. Not forever. She knew that. But it was still pretty amazing to contemplate the idea that Larkin Wolff enjoyed making love to her.

Clearly, she was weak. This morning she had been 100 percent sure that she was never going to let it happen again. But all he had to do was touch her and she was seduced. She couldn't even blame it on Larkin, not really. She *wanted* to be persuaded. And that was the most sobering realization of all.

Moments later, a house came into view. It was tucked back into the woods in such a way that it resembled a storybook dwelling. Larkin pointed to the right of the clearing where an enormous oak reached toward the sky. "My cousin Kieran spent much of his career building things all over the globe. Now that he's a family man, he still needs to get his creative kicks somehow. So Cammie has the world's coolest tree house. She won't mind us taking a look."

They clambered up a narrow ladder, and Winnie's eyes widened as she took it all in. "This is incredible." Cammie's dad had built the tree house on four levels, each connected by ladders or walkways. A child's touch was evident in the small furnishings and the assortment of toys and clothing tossed about.

Larkin took her hand. "C'mon. We're going all the way to the top. Cammie is not allowed up here without her mom or dad." The final ladder was barely wide enough to accommodate an adult's hips. And the angle made it an almost vertical climb.

Winnie's knees weakened with a tinge of vertigo when she glanced over the side. Here in the leafy canopy, the ground looked very far away. At this final level, the breeze was cool. Not only that, but tucked up against a reassuringly steady rail sat a small settee covered in cheerful chintz.

Larkin grinned at her. "I suspect that my cousin and his wife use this as a romantic rendezvous from time to time. But who knows." He leaned back on the tree trunk, smiling as Winnie kicked off her shoes and sat down. "Did you ever have a tree house as a kid?"

"No. I don't think my parents were that whimsical."

"Too bad." He fell silent, and she saw a shadow slide over his face. It might have been the wind moving leaves above him, or it might have been a painful recollection.

It turned out that the latter was true.

Larkin shoved his hands in his pockets, the set of his mouth grim. "I decided that I owe it to you to explain about my father."

"You don't. Really you don't." She had her own guilty secrets, and if Larkin started spilling his, she might face a moral obligation to do the same. That thought petrified her.

He ignored her assurance, his gaze trained on the forest, seeing things Winnie couldn't see. Finally, he broke the silence.

"You asked about my relationship with my dad. It's complicated. You picked up on that the first night. Devlyn and Annalise and I respect our father, and I guess you could say we love him, but things are strained."

She decided to stay silent. Larkin didn't appear to expect any comment.

He continued, but perhaps he was not aware of how tightly his hands gripped the railing at his sides. "Before we came to Wolff Mountain, both our families lived in Charlottesville in big, impressive, side-by-side houses. Dad and Uncle Victor were twenty years older than the women they married. I think the wives were friends. I was too young to really evaluate that. But on the day they disappeared, they were out shopping together."

"The kidnapping." She had read most of the details, but it seemed important for Larkin to retell it, so she listened.

"Despite the fact that my father and uncle paid the ransom, both of the women were shot and killed execution style. Looking at it now, from the perspective of almost thirty years later, I think the authorities must have bungled the case, but the end result was the same. My mother and my aunt were dead. And their killers were never apprehended."

"So you all came to the mountain."

"Well, not at first. It took nine months to build Wolff Castle. We were shuffled back and forth with private security guards. Victor and Vincent wanted us to get used to the idea of our new home. Which was a good thing, because when we got here we were prisoners, essentially."

"Because they were afraid the same thing would happen to you."

"Yes." He glanced at her, his eyes bleak. "The level of collective grief was monumental. It's amazing we all survived and grew up to be functional adults. My dad and my uncle were in a daze for a couple of years. We had nannies and tutors who kept things going on a daily basis."

"So you resented your father for not being there for you?"

His smile held little humor. "Don't try to psychoanalyze this, Winnie. The truth is much darker. Devlyn and Annalise and I were thrilled to be here on the mountain. And guilty as hell because we felt reborn. Our mother was an abusive alcoholic who liked slapping and hitting and…" His throat worked, and he turned away for a moment, ostensibly to brush away a cricket that had landed on his arm.

When he looked at her again, Winnie saw a lifetime of grief that was so deep and dark it made her want to weep. "You don't have to tell me this," she whispered.

He shrugged. "It was a long time ago. Our aunt Laura was a saint to us. When my mom was drinking we would run next door and she would try to keep us occupied. And you have to remember, Annalise was a toddler, and I was not in kindergarten yet. It was Devlyn who bore the brunt of it."

"But why?" she cried softly, her chest hurting. "Could your aunt not intervene?"

"She was young. Probably in awe of her much older husband. And maybe back then, people were more likely to turn a blind eye. I don't know. But what I do know is that I failed my brother and my sister, and that tore me up, even as a kid. I slipped into Devlyn's bedroom one night after our mother had been on a rampage. He was huddled under his blankets, crying, trying to put medicine and Band-Aids on the places where she had burned him with a cigarette."

"Oh, my God." Winnie's stomach pitched in horror.

"When I tried to talk to him, he just waved me away. We never spoke of it. My job was to keep Annalise out of sight. And for some reason, that worked."

"Then how did you fail her?"

"A little girl needs her mother. I tried to find times when my mother wasn't drinking. I'd brush Annalise's hair and help her put on a pretty dress. I thought if our mom was sober she'd want to play with her little daughter. But she was too self-absorbed to notice. So Annalise felt that rejection. She says she doesn't remember much about those early years, but I know it marked her. It took her a long, long time to trust anyone enough to get married."

Winnie swallowed, too invested in the story to quit now. "And your father did nothing?"

"Well, that's the thing…he told Devlyn a while back that he never knew. That he was working long hours to make a living, and was seldom at home when we were awake. He apologized to Devlyn. And we've forgiven him, I suppose. But the emotional damage that was done to all three of us can't just be wiped away. Our dad is our dad. But there aren't any warm, fuzzy feelings between us."

"I'm sorry." She didn't know what else to say. She wanted to cry for the little boy. But not in front of the man he had become.

Sixteen

Larkin studied Winnie's face. The rustling leaves dappled her cheeks with shards of sunlight. She had curled her legs into a pretzel position, and the familiar posture caused a memory of the night before to flash in front of his eyes. Though Winnie was wearing more clothes at the moment, she was no less alluring.

Her pale skin reminded him of an Irish beauty. Slim legs and arms had developed a pink flush, either from the sun or from the heat of the day. The tank top she wore outlined her lush curves, and her shorts were long enough to be modest, but short enough to make him crazy. Her wonderful, riotous, pale gold hair was caught up in a ponytail on the back of her head. Renegade wisps curled around her face.

What he felt for her was more than simple lust. But he couldn't articulate the difference. Never one to voluntarily spill his guts, he had now run out of things to say.

When the silence deepened, Winnie cocked her head. "Why

did you feel the need to tell me this? I didn't expect you to be so open with someone you've known for such a brief time."

He shrugged. "I want you to know why this whole responsibility thing is an issue with me. It's only been in the last couple of years—now that I see Devlyn and Annalise finally happy, really happy—that I've felt a load lifted. And I like that feeling. Watching people I love suffer was excruciating. Trying to help and being virtually useless. I can't go through that again. And long-term relationships carry that risk."

"You don't owe me any explanations."

"Maybe not. But I want to have honesty between us."

She looked down at her lap, moving her hands restlessly, rubbing her knees, swatting a fly... "I appreciate that."

He sat down beside her. "It's too pretty a day to waste being sad. I hope I haven't ruined it for you."

She grimaced. "It's not ruined. But I can't help grieving for all of you."

"You dealt with a pretty terrible loss yourself. And you made it through."

"I suppose."

She was more subdued than usual. He wondered if she was judging him for his failings or searching for any signs that he had his mother's tendencies. He put a hand under her chin. "Look at me, Winnie."

They were so close he could have counted the smattering of freckles on her cheeks if he'd been so inclined. But what he really wanted was a kiss. When Winnie kissed him, he felt invincible, as though he had won a rare prize.

She curled an arm around his neck. "Are we playing Tarzan and Jane?"

"I do like the thought of you in a leopard skin."

"Men. You're so easy."

"You don't find Tarzan sexy?"

"He was a hunter-gatherer. Women like being cared for."

"His rock-hard abs had nothing to do with it?"

"Mmm. I plead the fifth." She nuzzled his nose. "I like this tree house. Maybe I won't go back to Nashville. Maybe I'll stay right here where no one can find me."

"You wouldn't be able to forget about your flock. Admit it."

"True. But don't make it out to be some noble endeavor. I like being needed. So in a very real way, what I do is selfish."

He chuckled. "You'll never sell that one, Winnie. But nice try. And getting back to Tarzan…"

"Yes?" She uncurled her legs and leaned against him, her back to his chest.

His cheek came down to hers. "You said that women like being cared for. But it seems to me that you're the one who does all the caring. Who takes care of you?"

"My parents left me well cared for."

"I'm not talking about money, and you know it. What about relatives?"

"I told you that my parents were much older when they had me. So by the time I was in grade school, I had lost all four of my grandparents."

"Aunts…uncles?"

"My mom and dad were only children. I've always suspected that was what brought them together. Even when I was an older teenager, before they were killed, I didn't have the impression that their relationship was particularly passionate. They were more like friends who had never had siblings, so they found something valuable in their working collaboration."

"And your friends?"

"You tell me. Aren't your siblings and cousins your best friends?"

He frowned. "Yes. So what?"

"I wasn't lucky enough to have such a *band of brothers*. And I was much like you in that I had tutors at home. College was not a great experience, because I was too gawky and shy to be comfortable with the students who came from backgrounds like mine and too wealthy to fit in with kids who were

living on ramen noodles. I've always kept to myself. I do have
women who mean something to me and whom I trust, but our
connection is more about the work we do than anything personal. But it's okay. I don't mind taking care of myself. That
was a lesson I learned early."

Something moved inside him, an inescapable emotion that
tightened his throat and made him want to give her everything
she had missed. Even strong people needed a human connection to sustain them. Winnie cared for so many, but it wasn't the
type of equal relationship that offered something to her, as well.

He shifted her and twined his hand in her ponytail, pulling
back her head for a long, lazy kiss. Gradually he was learn-
ing what she liked, what made her sigh, what made her melt.
"Trust me now, Winnie." Without waiting for permission, he
unfastened her bra and stripped it and her top over her head.

"Larkin," she objected. "What are you doing?"

"Relax," he said, palming her breasts and bouncing them
lightly. "No one can see us." It was true. The spring foliage
was already dense, so no one could spot them from the ground.
And if anyone started up the lowest ladder, the noise would
give Larkin and Winnie plenty of time to compose themselves.

Winnie closed her eyes, her breath coming in jerky pants.
Her breasts were beautiful, full and ripe and delicious. He bent
his head to kiss one raspberry nipple. Last night he'd barely
caught a glimpse of her. This afternoon, in the unforgiving
light of day, she was impossibly alluring. His hands shook
and his mouth dried.

"Stand up, honey."

With Winnie looking at him, big-eyed, he removed her socks
and shoes and then gently stripped her shorts and underwear
down slim, firm legs. Leaving her to her own devices a moment, he pulled his shirt over his head, unzipped his jeans and
pushed his pants and boxers to his knees. His erection sprang
forth, hungry and tall.

Winnie's mesmerized stare did wonders for his ego. He

grabbed a condom from his pocket and rolled it on. "Come here, Jane," he said with a grin. That was something new. Humor and lust all in one moment. Winnie made him smile, even when he was so damned aroused, he ached from head to toe.

She raised an eyebrow. "There's no room to lie down."

"We're not going to lie down." Her look of dawning surprise swamped him with tenderness. He took her wrist and pulled her forward to straddle his hips. The sun-warmed cushion at his back felt welcoming. But when Winnie lowered herself onto him, hands braced on his shoulders, he felt at home. As though every dark shadow that had ever cloaked Wolff Mountain suddenly floated away on the breeze.

Her tight passage gripped him, causing sweat to break out on his forehead. The snug fit was incredible, making his head swim. He gripped her ass, trying not to lose control. "God, Winnie. I can't get enough of you." Slowly, he began to move. She caught his rhythm immediately, lifting and lowering in a lazy dance.

She inhaled sharply when he changed angles.

"You like that?"

She nodded, mute.

He buried his face between her breasts and inhaled the warm scent of her skin. No woman had ever made him feel like this, young and carefree, as though all of his past had been erased and life consisted of only this one perfect moment.

Sliding his hands up to her waist, he rocked her, feeling the way her thighs pressed against his, hearing the way her breathing labored as he drove her higher.

"Say something," he muttered. His bed partners were usually more vocal. Winnie's silence piqued him, made him wonder what she was thinking.

She bounced experimentally, and he cursed as the added stimulation sent him careening toward the end. "Winnie…"

"Can't speak…finish it…" She leaned to one side, took his

earlobe in her teeth and nipped it hard enough to make him shiver as the combination of pain and pleasure shot through his veins like a drug.

His arms locked around her waist, his hips thrust upward and he gave a muffled shout as his climax grabbed him without warning and tumbled him in a never-ending wave. Winnie came, too. He heard and felt her release. But after that, all he could do was slump into the sofa and try to remember how to breathe.

Winnie's bottom was cold. And the muscles in her legs trembled. She lay sprawled on top of Larkin in a position that could only be described as immodest. But she couldn't find the strength to care. Larkin's heart thudded beneath her cheek, the beat steady, strong.

The euphoria of physical release faded as she acknowledged the painful truth. She had fallen in love with a lone Wolff. Holding him now, with no one to see, no one to care, was the most exquisite pleasure she'd ever experienced. Everything about him was admirable. In the faces of his family she saw love and respect for him. Even back in Nashville she had noted the caliber of his employees and the deference with which they spoke to him.

How would she ever be able to walk away? But she had no choice. It wasn't as if she could stay and fight. He had told her from the beginning that he liked his life as it was. And if she truly cared for him, she would do the right thing and leave. No regrets. Surely a man who had suffered as much as Larkin had growing up deserved a time of peace.

His hand toyed with her hair, curling it around his fingers. When his fingers brushed her neck, she shivered. "Shouldn't we get dressed before someone discovers us?" she said.

He tickled her lower back. "I don't think I can move." The deep, drugged satisfaction in the words told her that he had felt the same incredible connection that still bound them both physically and otherwise.

Clumsily, she levered herself up and off him. With his tousled hair, his bare chest and his…um…manly parts on display, he looked like what he was, a charming, sinfully attractive multimillionaire. It was odd, though, that she seldom thought of Larkin as being wealthy. His down-to-earth approach to life matched hers. And she liked that about him.

Though she tried to dress quickly, Larkin's appreciative scrutiny made her hands fumble. Her underwear ended up inside out, but she left it that way, anxious to be fully clothed. At last, he stood up, dealt with the condom and readjusted his boxers and pants. He yawned and stretched. His chest was beautiful…smooth and tanned and rippled with sleek muscles. A thin line of hair bisected his chest and ran down to his belt buckle. She knew how silky that hair was, and where it led.

Sitting on the settee to put on her shoes, she looked up at him. "We promised we'd help decorate. I don't want your sister sending out a search party."

"You're right." He shrugged into his shirt and ran his hands through his short hair. "We might as well get it over with." He reached for her one more time and kissed her forehead. "But tonight you're mine—right?"

Winnie laughed ruefully. "After what happened just now, do you really think I'll say no to you later?"

Larkin's grin was wicked. He squeezed her butt. "Who knows? Women are capricious creatures."

Winnie wasn't about to get into a battle she was destined to lose. Already today she had let him talk her into sex when she'd been convinced it was a bad idea. She really didn't have a leg to stand on.

Larkin insisted on descending the ladder first. Which meant his big arms surrounded her as she backed down. Thus giving him a far-too-close vantage point of her legs and other parts. When she stood on the landing, his eyes were hot. "What if

I can't wait until tonight?" He backed her into the ladder, his hips anchoring hers. "It won't take long."

She realized he was serious. And his need and hunger did something to her insides. A combination of smug happiness and desperate yearning filled her like a helium balloon. For a man like Larkin Wolff to want her so badly healed a few of the rough edges of her youthful pain.

Before she could answer one way or the other, a man's voice sounded from below. "I know you're up there. Come on, you two. Annalise is breathing fire because we're all late."

Winnie looked down, way down, at the top of Kieran's head. "We're coming," she called, tugging at Larkin's hand and heading for the next ladder.

"I *would* have been coming," he groused, his voice pitched low enough so only she could hear. "If he hadn't interrupted."

"Behave," Winnie whispered. "This will be fun."

Decorating the outdoor tent for Sam's birthday was definitely a family affair. The weather couldn't have been more perfect, and the forecast for Saturday was identical. This was a milestone birthday for Sam, so Annalise had bought every inch of black crepe paper in Virginia, or so it seemed. There were balloons to blow up, satin ribbon swags to design and hang, and all around the room, black-and-white photos of Sam. Sam as a kid with his dad at Wolff Mountain, Sam on his college graduation day and one poignant picture of Sam standing with the Wolff boys in front of the castle. Annalise appeared just in the edge of the picture, her gaze trained on the man she would one day marry.

Even though Annalise could have been only sixteen or seventeen when the photo was shot, the heart-wrenching look on her face was entirely adult. The naked emotion in her eyes was one Winnie understood all too well. In fact, the picture made her so uncomfortable she turned her back on it and walked away to another part of the tent.

Devlyn Wolff joined her as she assembled small posies of

white roses and tucked them into ebony lacquer vases that would serve as table centerpieces. To her surprise, he pretended to help her, though his big hands mutilated the flowers. "I think you'd better let me do this," she said, waving him off.

He perched on top of the table where she was working, his feet propped on a chair. A big, handsome man, he exuded charm and sex appeal, though Winnie was immune. As the head of Wolff Enterprises, his responsibilities were legion, yet here he was in the midst of a family gathering, seemingly content to be frittering away a Friday afternoon.

He handed her a tiny black ribbon she had dropped. "You do realize that my brother has never brought a woman here before."

Winnie shot him a glance. "So I've heard."

"You must have made an impression on him. This is his private space."

"Your brother is a kind, generous man. I needed a place to hide out, and he offered to bring me here."

"He went through a bimbo phase in college and shortly after."

Winnie grinned. "I've heard that, too. Trust me. I won't do anything to harm your baby brother."

Every ounce of humor disappeared from his face. "It's you I'm worried about, Winnie. I don't want to see you get hurt."

"Everyone keeps telling me that, including Larkin. It's okay. I get it. We're just having fun." She added that last part because surely the Wolffs were smart enough to realize something was going on. His family seemed to know him better than he realized.

Devlyn glanced across the chaos that was the large white tent where Sam's party would take place. "He takes too much upon himself. Tries to fix things that aren't his to fix."

"He told me a little about your childhood. Before the mountain. It hurt me to hear it, but I suppose you realize it's still fresh on his mind."

"It is for me and Annalise, too," he said, his gaze focused on something far away that she couldn't see. "I don't think you ever really forget something like that. We've grown up. And figured out that few families resemble a Norman Rockwell painting. Annalise and I have been lucky enough to find partners who love us and accept who we are, scars and all."

"But…"

He shrugged. "But Larkin suffered in different ways than I did. Emotional trauma can be as bad or worse than the physical."

She was well aware of that. "He's made a good life for himself."

"Alone."

"Yes."

"So you're aware of the danger."

"I could fall in love with him, and he could walk away."

"Exactly."

Winnie finished the last of the vases and began filling them with water. "I appreciate your concern, Devlyn—I really do. But I'm not the naive person I may appear to be. I understand Larkin better than you think. So thanks for the warning, but I'm okay."

He set the chair aside and stood up. "I wish I could be more encouraging. You fit in here on the mountain."

She arched her back, stretching out the kinks, hands on her hips. "I always knew my relationship with Larkin was a fleeting thing. He envies you all, I think. But not enough to take on the burden of marriage."

"Marriage isn't a burden."

"Maybe not for you."

"Take care of yourself, and take care of him."

"What if those two things are mutually exclusive?"

Devlyn flicked her ponytail. "You're a smart woman. Figure it out."

Seventeen

Larkin stood atop a wobbly ladder, winding little white lights around the central tent pole. His stomach pitched when Annalise, below him, accidentally bumped his perch. Heights made him queasy, and he was anxious to get this job done. It hadn't escaped his notice that Winnie and his brother were getting very chummy.

When he clambered back down to terra firma, Annalise beamed at him. "Thanks, bro."

His baby sister was happy all the time these days. And her sharp-edged tongue had mellowed considerably. It was a disconcerting, but enjoyable change. "You might want to rein in our sibling," he said. "He seems to be flirting with Winnie."

"Jealous much?" Annalise snorted. "If Gillian isn't concerned, why should I be?"

"Forget I mentioned it," he said grumpily. "Give me another string of lights and help me move this ladder."

By dinnertime Larkin was like a cat on hot bricks. The day had turned into one long *pre*-celebration. The entire family converged at the main house after the decorating, and didn't leave. The children were included at tonight's meal. Which meant that adult conversation was limited in favor of laughing at the antics of a toddler and an infant.

Little Cammie took her role as older cousin very seriously, and jumped up time and again to retrieve baby spoons, pick up toys and rescue Cheerios before they were ground into the priceless Oriental rug that ran the length and width of the dining room.

Larkin bantered back and forth with his relatives, all the while keeping a covert eye on Winnie. She was holding her own. The semi-organized insanity of a Wolff family meal was not for the faint of heart. But Winnie's shyness had melted away amid the unselfconscious joie de vivre of the evening's reunion.

As he surveyed the room, Larkin marveled inwardly at how far they had come as a family. Tragedy had brought them to this place, but love and acceptance kept them here.

He touched Winnie's knee beneath the Irish linen tablecloth, leaning over to be heard as he whispered in her ear. "Not exactly dinner at a five-star restaurant, is it?"

She smiled at him. "I adore your family," she said. "I stand by what I said earlier. You're a very lucky man."

"They like you." He wanted to say more than that, but he was still processing the words and feelings in his head.

"I like them, too. I'm so glad you brought me to the mountain." She was wearing another dress that made him sweat. Tonight's meal was more casual, and Winnie had chosen her wardrobe accordingly. But the cheerful halter-necked sundress in black-and-white check with appliquéd daisies left a lot of bare skin on display.

He draped an arm across the back of her chair, running his fingers lightly over the nape of her neck. "Are you wearing anything under that outfit?"

She lowered her voice, her attention ostensibly still on the table at large. "Why don't you find out?"

Her teasing question made him choke. He took a sip of wine, wiped his mouth with his napkin and moved his fingers three inches up her thigh. Winnie's virtually inaudible whimper hardened his sex instantly.

He'd had some bad ideas in his life, but this one ranked right up there at the top. Even so, to remove his hand from her smooth, bare leg was impossible. Winnie was seated to his left, so he was able to use his right hand to maintain the fiction of eating. Any interest he'd had in food had evaporated long ago.

Gradually, making sure no one could see, he inched his hand upward. A flush broke out on Winnie's fair cheeks, but she didn't react otherwise. He found the lacy edge of her panties and grinned, barely moving his lips as he leaned his head toward hers and mouthed in her ear. "I knew it. You're such a good little girl. No going commando for you."

Victor Wolff, seated in his usual spot at the head of the table, eyed them with a gimlet stare. "Enough of that, Larkin Wolff. Behave yourself. Quit whispering sweet nothings in Winnie's ear."

Larkin straightened abruptly and put both his hands on the table. He felt his own neck heat. For a moment there, he'd thought the old man had X-ray vision.

Winnie was visibly amused at his mortification. "Busted," she murmured as she leaned down to pick up the napkin that Larkin's antics had dislodged.

Larkin wiped a hand over his damp forehead. He couldn't take much more of this. When he glanced at his watch, he saw that it was almost eight-thirty. Dessert was just being served... pound cake with imported strawberries and fresh cream. His favorite.

He shoved his chair from the table and stood up. The big group was so rowdy, he had to shout twice. "Hey. Hey, you crazy people."

Finally, all heads turned in his direction. He cleared his

throat. "Winnie and I have really enjoyed hanging out with everyone today, but I promised her a walk to Wolff Point tonight."

Winnie looked up at him. "But we—"

He kicked her foot. "So if you'll excuse us, we'll say goodnight and see everyone in the morning."

The chorus of goodbyes and teasing innuendos was neverending. By the time he got Winnie out into the hallway, he was breathing hard.

She tugged on his arm. "What was that all about? You took me to Wolff Point last night. Are we going again?"

In the front hallway, he caught a glimpse of his face in the ornate mirror over the console table. His eyes glittered with feverish intent. Staring down at the woman who had turned his world upside down, he shook his head, reeling from the revelations that came thick and fast.

"No," he said, his voice blunt and harsh. "I'm going to make love to you." God help him. And in thirty-six hours he was going to walk away. If he had the strength. Bringing her here had been a mistake. Because he'd now had a vision of how his life *could* be, but the consequences were unthinkable. If he gave in to the lure of Winnie's pure, sweet tenderness, he'd be committed. Forever. Imagining that responsibility scared him to the point of nausea. He couldn't love her and fail her. Love her and lose her. He'd rather endure the prospect of a sterile life alone, insulated from pain.

He knew love and he knew loss. His way was better. His way was the only choice.

Winnie trailed in his wake, propelled by his urgency. Despite the enjoyable family dinner, she was as eager to be alone, just the two of them, as Larkin seemed to be. He didn't waste time asking questions about location. Edging open her door with his hip, he dragged her inside.

Finally—a lock between them and the outside world—he

paused to catch his breath. The hands he ran up and down her arms held a slight tremor. "You were wrong," he muttered.

"About what?"

Larkin untied the small bow at the back of her neck and pulled the bodice of the dress to her waist. "God, you're gorgeous."

When he bent his head and took one of her nipples between his teeth, pleasure sparked through her veins and her knees wobbled. He caught her up against him with one strong arm across her back, kissing her wildly. She sensed a change in him, an urgency that went beyond mere passion.

Breaking free for a moment, she smoothed a hand over his cheek. "Wrong about what?"

"Marital bliss. Turns out it *is* contagious." His eyes were dark, his expression more so.

"You're not making sense," she said, waiting impatiently for him to finish removing her dress.

When she was down to nothing but her French-cut panties, he stopped and stared. "We have to talk."

Her nipples peaked, aching and hot. "About what?" The ferocity of his molten azure gaze might as well have been a physical caress. The tactile examination ran from her face to her belly and below. She shifted nervously from one foot to the other. Between her legs, her sex dampened, swelled, readied for him.

"I'm confused, but everything is getting clearer."

Nothing he said made sense. But she understood without words what he wanted. And the erection tenting the front of his slacks reinforced her conclusion.

"One of us is lagging behind." She was getting better at undressing him, but her fingers fumbled with the buttons at the cuffs of his dress shirt. He finally helped her and removed the rest of his clothing in an impatient one-footed dance.

Winnie clasped her hands between her breasts, trying to

keep her heart from punching through her chest. Larkin was the gorgeous one.

He took her hand. "Do you trust me, Winnie? To always tell you the truth?"

"I do." The sound of the vow made her wince inwardly, but Larkin didn't seem to notice.

He scooped her up in his arms and carried her to the bed. "I can't wait, baby. I'm sorry. We'll take the edge off and start all over again." Not bothering to peel back the sumptuous covers, he deposited her on the mattress and came down beside her, pausing only to take care of protection. As he moved between her legs, she arched into his thrust, groaning as he filled her completely. The sense of connection, of utter rightness, stole her breath.

His skin was damp against hers, the muscles in his arms cording as he held his weight on his hands. Moving his hips first lazily, then with more force, he took her further and faster than before. She wanted to savor the moment. To tuck it away and remember it in the days ahead when he would no longer be part of her everyday life.

But there was no time for reflection, no opportunity for even a fleeting rational thought. Larkin had learned what pleased her, and he used the knowledge to advantage. Again and again he drove her to the edge, taking her close, but never letting her fall.

It was agony and perfection. Torture and bliss.

His eyes were closed now, unwittingly shutting her out. With his skin drawn tightly across sharp cheekbones, he breathed harshly, raggedly. He was completely in control, his strength and power present in every thrust.

She wrapped her legs around his waist, driving him deeper still. And then it was upon them…without warning…a spine-numbing, breath-stealing surge of release that left her with no recourse but to grip his slick, powerful shoulders and hold on until the end.

* * *

Larkin was sleeping. And no wonder. The second time he'd taken her, the devil of a man had drawn out the wanting, the claiming, the exquisite joining. He'd moved inside her for what seemed like hours, his hands and lips coaxing her once again to a heated pitch of wanting that made her lose all sense of reason.

Now she lay on her side facing him. She had gone to the bathroom, used the facilities and washed up. He never stirred.

Lightly brushing the hair on his arm, she tried to analyze his words. *You were wrong. Marital bliss is contagious. We need to talk.*

A less pragmatic woman might coax herself into believing that Larkin Wolff was leading up to a proposal. But Winifred Bellamy was smarter than that. Throat tight, she glanced at the clock. It was still early...not quite midnight. She wasn't sleepy. Her head buzzed with unformed thoughts, amorphous daydreams.

She would make Larkin Wolff a good wife. If he wanted one. But that idea was so dangerous, she locked it away rapidly, reaching for her usual steady footing. Life was good. She was blessed in many ways. She didn't need a man to be complete.

Suddenly, her cell phone on the nightstand buzzed. She had it set to vibrate, but even so, it was loud. Sliding from beneath the covers, she grabbed it up and answered it in a low voice. "Hello..."

Larkin jerked awake, every sense on high alert. A sharp sound had dragged him out of a deep sleep. Groggy, he glanced around, identified his surroundings as Winnie's bedroom and sat up. Immediately, he knew what had awakened him. Because it happened a second time. A keening, stricken cry that brought the hair on his arms to attention.

He bounded out of bed, not even taking time to turn on the light, and crouched beside her. She was huddled on her knees in the midst of the carpeted floor, arms wrapped around her waist. Tears streamed down her face as she rocked back and forth.

"Lord, honey. What's wrong?" He had never seen his strong, unbreakable Winnie like this, and the change shocked him. Gathering her into his arms, he sat cross-legged with her in his lap, cuddling her, stroking her back, smoothing his hand over her hair. "Tell me, Winnie."

He had a long wait. She seemed unable to stem the outpouring of grief, and his mind raced with possibilities, each one worse than the last.

Her skin was icy, even with his arms wrapped around her.

When she finally spoke, he could barely understand her. Her teeth chattered, and her words were choppy. "Esteban's father killed his mother and grandmother."

Larkin reeled, his stomach pitching with nausea. "Dear God. Are you sure? Don't answer that. Of course you're sure. Dear God." His mouth dried as horror congealed everything inside him that had life and breath. "I promised him that he and his mother would be safe. That he didn't have to be afraid." Leland *Security*. What an ass he was, thinking he could protect people. What an unmitigated ass. He couldn't keep anyone safe.

Winnie burrowed her face into his chest, making her speech even further garbled. "Not your fault. She left the property. He killed her first and then himself." Fresh sobs shook her small frame.

Larkin gathered her up and put her back to bed. He retrieved a wet washcloth from the bathroom and wiped her face gently. She lay on her back, staring dully at the canopy atop the bed. The lovely room was not a fit setting for such raw, unimaginable news.

He felt the old feelings of failure claw at his chest, and had he not been a man, he might have joined Winnie in her cathartic tears. Seeing her pain and being unable to do anything about it destroyed him. "How did she get out?"

Winnie turned her head to stare at him. Light streamed from

the bathroom, illuminating the bed. She was pale, too pale, and every freckle stood out in relief against her colorless skin. "The mothers and children aren't prisoners," she said huskily. "We have nothing or no one to tell them they can't leave. They are given extensive counseling and cautioned again and again never to meet alone with an abusive husband or boyfriend. But they want so badly to believe a man can change, *their* man in particular, that they'll sometimes do anything he asks."

He tried to wrap his brain around the story she was telling. But he felt sick and guilty. "How did he find her?"

Winnie slung an arm over her face, covering her eyes. "He broke out of jail. Tortured the grandmother until she gave him a cell number. After killing the grandmother, he called Esteban's mom. Begged for forgiveness. Asked to talk, just talk. She told him where to meet her…thank God, not at the actual address. Then she left my property and walked two miles down the road. A car pulled up. He got out. Gunned her down. Put the gun in his mouth. There were witnesses."

Winnie rolled to her belly as a fresh wave of sobs threatened to tear her in half. Larkin sat like stone, his mind barely functioning as he remembered Esteban's oddly adult eyes but unquenchable cheer.

Suddenly Larkin was back in his childhood. He heard Devlyn cry out once. It was never more than once. She would take him by surprise and get that one shout of pain. After that, silence. Larkin huddled in a closet, Annalise in his arms. Her young voice was high-pitched, too loud. *Hush, sis. We don't have to stay here long. Let me braid your hair. Lean on me and fall asleep….*

"I have to go."

He snapped back to the present at the sound of Winnie's voice, his senses befuddled. "Go where?"

"Home." She climbed out of bed and started dressing. "Esteban is asking for me. They were going to take him into protective custody, but he begged to stay at the safe house. He has a support system there, so they allowed it. For the moment."

He rolled to the edge of the mattress and stood up, struggling for composure. Winnie had weathered the storm and was visibly pulling herself together with a strength of will Larkin admired deeply. "We'll take the jet," he said gruffly. "Once you're ready, we can be at the airstrip in forty-five minutes."

Winnie whirled to look at him. Her hair was a mess. Dark smudges underscored her eyes. "You are not going," she said flatly. "Your family needs you here today. They deserve that."

Fury rushed over him with the heat of a thousand suns. "And what do *you* deserve, Winnie? You hired me to keep your little enclave safe."

"And you did. Admirably. But one of my women broke the rules and paid for it with her life. Any way you slice it, it's not your battle."

"This isn't up for discussion." He reached around her and turned on the lamp. He was still nude, but he didn't care.

Winnie glared at him. "Your entire family, every one of them, is gathered here to celebrate your brother-in-law's birthday. It would be unforgivable of you to disappoint them."

His fists clenched to keep from pulling her into his arms. "You need someone, Winnie. Someone to stand beside you during all of this."

She froze, her arms holding a stack of clothes to be tucked into her suitcase. "Don't say that. This is my problem, my responsibility. I can handle it."

"I know you can *handle* it, damn it. But you're not going to. We're in this together."

"No, I…" Her chin wobbled. She didn't have it in her to fight him. No reserves left at all. Which, he surmised, was the only reason he won the argument.

"Finish getting ready. I'll call the pilot and get dressed. I'll be back in less than ten minutes."

* * *

They left the house in silence, and silence reigned for the entire trip from Wolff Castle to the airstrip. Larkin drove. It meant he had to keep his attention on the road. He wanted badly to comfort Winnie in the only way he knew how, but this was neither the time nor the place for what he had in mind.

On the jet, he thought she would immediately fall asleep. Instead, she kicked off her shoes and tucked her legs beneath her, choosing a seat opposite his. They were served a small snack during preflight checks and taxiing. Once they were airborne, Larkin requested pillows and blankets from the attendant and then asked not to be disturbed.

Winnie was a broken flower stem, her head drooping with fatigue. He didn't know what to say to her. Even now, his *wanting* to help was not enough. It never had been.

She stared at him, her gold-and-green eyes hazed with grief. "I don't think you should be here. But I'm selfish enough to be glad you are."

His hands clenched the armrests. "I wouldn't be anywhere else. My sister and all the rest of them will understand."

"I hope so. You've been more than good to me, Larkin. Don't ever think differently. And though you don't realize it, you've brought me out of a long, deep freeze. You asked me why I do what I do. I think you deserve to know."

Shock immobilized him for the tick of several seconds. Then he pulled up the two armrests and beckoned her. "Come sit with me, Winnie. You're too far away."

She did as he asked. In moments her head was in his lap, the rest of her curled like a child in the cramped length of the two extra seats. He stroked her hair, torn between wanting her to rest and the need to hear the secret she had been unable or unwilling to share before now.

So he waited.

When he put his right arm around her waist, she linked her fingers with his. "It happened when my parents died," she said, her words drowsy and slow. "Our family lawyer was a man in his early forties. He was so kind to me, so helpful after the tsunami. There were arrangements to be made, decisions to wade through. I wanted to jump on a plane and go there. He convinced me that it would be best to stay home. After photos and videos began to pour in, I knew he was right."

"But you said the bodies were recovered?"

"Eventually. I had known the lawyer for years as Mr. Parker. He now insisted I call him Mike. And during the funerals, everything…he was right there, holding my hand…literally. I don't know what I would have done without him."

Larkin's left hand fisted at his side. This wasn't going to be good. "And afterward?"

"He came around a lot. Sometimes even spent the night, always with an excuse about it being too late to drive back into town. I didn't think a thing about it."

"But something changed." Hearing her recitation was tearing him asunder, because he had a fair guess as to what was coming.

"Yes," she said. "Something changed. One night after dinner, after the housekeeper left, Mike sat down with me in the living room. Told me he wanted to talk about my future. I told him what I was thinking. That I wanted to travel a bit…perhaps get an advanced degree. Then he…"

"Then he what?"

"I had been crying. About my parents. So he kissed me. At first I thought he was just being nice. Trying to make me feel better. But he put his hand on my breast."

"Goddamn it to hell." Even forewarned, Larkin wasn't able to mask his reaction.

Winnie's whole body tensed beneath his hand. His instinctive outburst had upset her. He clenched his jaw, his breathing shallow.

"I'm sorry, love." He touched her cheek. "Go on." If he had to bite off his own tongue, he would listen impassively.

"I didn't know what to do. It made me uneasy. He was younger than my father, but still old enough to be my parent. It was weird."

"Did you ask him to stop?"

"I was confused and upset. Maybe I was overreacting. I knew absolutely zero about boys and even less about men. He—"

She stopped short, and Larkin saw that she was blushing, this time not from any kind of sexual pleasure...but from shame. He sat in silence, his heart in shreds, refusing to react so she could finish. But if he'd had his way, the man would be neutered by now.

He squeezed her hand. "It's okay, Winnie. You don't have to go through all the details."

She nodded against his leg. "Well, anyway, that went on for a long time—the touching, I mean—and then he undressed me. I know it makes me sound like the worst kind of ignorant fool, but I didn't realize what was going to happen. He had taken care of my every need for weeks. It was hard to believe that he would hurt me."

"But he did."

Another nod. "He took my virginity against my will. By the time I put up a serious protest, I couldn't make him stop. It wasn't particularly violent, just painful and terrifying."

Larkin shuddered, tears of fury in his eyes. He wiped them with the back of his hand. "I am so sorry." He could barely get out the words. The unimaginable horror of what she *wasn't* saying tormented him. And his brain filled in the rest.

When he thought he could speak calmly, he touched her eyelids, her nose, her soft, perfect lips. "Then what happened?"

"He went home. Said he would be back in the morning to talk. I found out later that he had a wife and kids waiting for him. I went upstairs and cried myself to sleep. I thought about calling the police, but I knew instinctively that he would deny anything had happened, or that he would spin the story and make me the supplicant. So I rested. And I waited."

"And in the morning?"

"He came back with legal papers. Told me that it would be in my best interests to let him control my money. That it was clear I was too young to make informed decisions. And that since we were now lovers, he would look out for me."

"What did you say?"

Winnie sat up, shoving her hair from her face with two hands. A tiny poignant smile brought back a fleeting hint of sunshine to her face. "I said no. He couldn't believe it. I accused him of raping me. Even in the state I was in, I had enough sense not to let him rationalize what had happened. I was in shock, I know. Too muddled to realize that I should have called the authorities even knowing it would be my word against his. But I told him to leave and never come back. I don't know where I found the courage, but I think I surprised him."

"Because he was expecting you to fall in line."

Winnie grimaced. "Yes."

"Damn," Larkin said gruffly. "You are one amazing woman. But I'm guessing he didn't take that well." He let her see his admiration, but not his loathing for her attacker. She had refused to be a victim and he would do all in his power to protect that heartbreaking dignity.

"He did not. First, he tried to undress me again. I kneed him in the groin. Then he tried threats. I laughed at him."

"Ouch."

"He said some pretty awful things about how no man would ever want me after what had happened and that I was hopeless when it came to sex. For a long time afterward, I believed him."

"Bastard…"

"Then he threw me into a wall and broke my jaw."

"Jesus."

They stared at each other, Winnie's gaze wary, her arms wrapped around her waist. She shrugged. "He stormed out. I think the blood scared him. I called an ambulance and ended up having surgery. When it was all over, I found a decent lawyer and filed charges. Mike is now serving an extended sentence in a federal pen."

"I wish I believed in the death penalty," Larkin growled, meaning every word. The thought of a young, defenseless Winnie being sexually assaulted and abused shoved his anger to catatonic levels.

"The point is," she said quietly, "that because I was reared in a good family, well educated and left with plenty of money, I had the self-confidence to do what I did. And the courage to do so, because I had options. Choices. The women I work with have none of that. So they stay in abusive relationships longer than they should…sometimes far too long. So now you see why I have to help."

He bowed his head momentarily, feeling something that was far stronger than pity, much deeper than compassion.

"Thank you for telling me," he said quietly. "We have about a half hour before we land. Why don't you lie back down and try to sleep."

When Winnie closed her eyes, he heard her breathing grow deep and steady in moments. He knew that telling him her deepest secret had exhausted her emotionally. And coming on the heels of what had happened to Esteban's mother, he suspected the recounting of her own experience of violence had drained her to the point of collapse.

His reaction to the truth was a physical pain that permeated every cell of his being. Though it made no sense, he felt guilty that he had been unable to save her. And what about now? Who would be there to keep her from harm in the years ahead? He couldn't, wouldn't answer the question. Not if he wanted to survive.

When Winnie walked into the safe house a couple of hours later, the women encircled her, their faces filled with relief. Despite the elaborate security precautions put in place by Larkin and his team, these vulnerable, terrified wives and girlfriends and mothers found solace in Winnie's presence.

She had made Larkin promise to stay outside until she summoned him.

The crowd parted and Esteban stepped forward. "*Hola, Miss Winnie. I missed you.*" He burst into tears as she knelt and gathered him into her arms. Every set of eyes in the room was wet.

Winnie rocked him in a tight embrace as she whispered to him. "Everything will be okay, my sweet boy. Don't you worry."

At last he pulled away, wiped his face on his sleeve and looked at her. "Señor Lobo?" he asked hopefully.

Winnie smiled. "Right outside. You want to go with me to see him?"

"*Sí, sí...*"

In the yard, Winnie stood back, unable to stem more tears, as Larkin swooped up the child and held him in strong arms. The two males carried on a low-voiced conversation she couldn't hear, but something Larkin said actually coaxed a laugh from Esteban.

Larkin smiled. "I explained to Esteban that you've been awake all night and need to sleep. He's going to play here today with his friends, and I promised you'd be back to see him this evening."

Winnie nodded, barely able to stand. "Sounds good to me."

At the house, she allowed Larkin to pamper her. He carried her up to her bedroom and set her on her feet. "A shower?"

She nodded. "But with you."

The conflict on his face was unmistakable. "I don't want to—"

She put a hand over his mouth. "Do this for me. Please. Wash me. Make love to me. Sleep with me."

But despite her begging, Larkin had his own agenda. He touched her as if she were a priceless, fragile treasure. As he bathed her in the shower, his sex was erect and demanding. Larkin, however, paid no attention to anything but her comfort. When she swayed with exhaustion, he dried her off, sat her on a low stool and combed her hair, blow-drying it as he went, until her unruly tresses lay docile on her shoulders.

He seemed to have a desire to carry her, so for once, she let herself be weak. When he tucked her into bed, she put her hand on his arm, feeling the warmth of him. "I need you," she said.

He hesitated. In his eyes, for a split second, she saw the truth. He was trying, but it was too much. This was exactly what Larkin *didn't* want. A clingy woman. A relationship that demanded he play the protector. *Oh, God.* "Never mind," she said hurriedly. "I'm fine." Somewhere she found the courage to smile. "Really I am. Please turn off the light as you go out."

Larkin's misery and distress and wretched guilt coalesced into a sharp, thrusting pain that stole his breath. "You should rest, Winnie."

The look on her face hurt him more than anything he had ever faced. Every hint of color remaining in her pale cheeks faded away, leaving her gaze dull with acceptance. "I understand. You can go home. I'll handle this. I don't need you. It's okay."

Dear God. She was trying to let him off the hook. Acknowledging his total inability to support her emotionally. Words failed him. Everything he had ever believed about himself splintered in a silent roar of agony. All he had to do was climb into that bed and hold her, but if he did, his heart would break. Nothing he could say or do would fix the situation with Esteban. Nothing he had to offer would take away Winnie's pain. "I'm sorry," he muttered. "I'm sorry." He turned blindly toward the door and walked out.

* * *

Winnie awoke alone and disoriented. She was actually hungry, and no wonder. She had slept for three hours. Afternoon sun lit the hardwood floor, catching dust motes in the slanted beams.

Reality washed over her. Brutal. Inescapable. It was hard to breathe. Esteban. Larkin. The pain was vast. Endless. Swinging her feet over the side of the bed, she stood up and put a hand on the wall when the room spun. How could she live? How could she move? The future gaped before her. Hollow. Terrifyingly empty.

Forcing herself to go through the motions, she freshened up and dressed. Her life was in ruins, but she wasn't the only one. Her responsibilities had not disappeared. Esteban needed her. Life had to go on. But first, something called out to her. The one place where she could funnel her heartbreak and perhaps find a measure of peace.

Larkin found her in the salon where they'd first met. Sitting at the beautiful piano. Her head was bent, her hands never slowing down. From what he remembered of his music-appreciation class, she was playing an incredibly difficult Chopin étude.

Her fingers flew over the keys. The notes rose and fell, filling the room, rich with beauty and sorrow and hope. He closed his eyes and let the music roll over him. How could a woman who had known so much tragedy in her life play with such joyous abandon?

He leaned against the wall, out of sight, eyes damp as he listened to what she couldn't or wouldn't say to him. When it was over, she closed the folio of sheet music and began to sob.

He couldn't bear it. "Don't, my love," he said. "Don't cry."

Her head snapped up, shock in every muscle as she wiped her face and composed herself. "You left."

"No," he said simply. "I didn't. I couldn't. I wouldn't. I've been walking the perimeter of the property, waiting for you to wake up."

Quietly, he sat down on the bench, facing the opposite direction. Not touching her.

She lifted her shoulders, her lips trembling, her spine straight. Wariness and disbelief filled her gaze. "Now I've played for you." She was wearing faded jeans and a gold Vanderbilt T-shirt that matched the amber in her eyes. On Wolff Mountain she had dressed the part of wealthy heiress. Today she was simply…Winnie. He liked both personas. But this was the woman who'd first caught his eye.

He put his arms around her, groaning when hers came around his waist and she rested her head on his shoulder. Sighing, he felt his world click into place. "How come you never told me you were a concert pianist?"

"Thirteen years of private lessons and a music minor in college. I hated every minute of it. Then when my parents died, I played out of guilt for months. One day I suddenly realized I loved the music. I had to get past all my childish rebellion to see what they had given me. A legacy of all the magnificent composers in the world. I'm a very lucky woman."

He nibbled her neck. "You're a very amazing woman. And I'm in love with you. Marry me, Winnie."

She jerked backward so fast they both nearly toppled off the bench. Hands clenched on his shoulders, she stared at him, eyes raw with grief. "That's not funny."

He kissed her nose. "No. It's damned serious. And while I'm at it, if Esteban has no other family members who can take him in, you and I might think about adopting him."

Tears leaked from her beautiful eyes, each one scoring him with regret for what he had done to her. His sins astounded him, but no more than his arrogance and insistence that he needed no one.

She put a hand on his forehead. "You didn't get any sleep last night. You're delirious."

"Never been saner."

"You loathe responsibility. You like a life that's footloose and fancy-free. You deserve that, Larkin. Really you do."

"I can't believe you ever slept with me. I was such an as—"

The hand moved from his forehead to cover his mouth. "You don't have to feel sorry for me. That's not why I told you my story on the plane."

"Do you feel sorry for *me?*"

"Well, I…" Her mouth opened and closed. "No," she said. "I don't."

"We've both lived through some horrific stuff. But I think we turned out pretty damned well."

She kept studying his eyes, as if expecting to read the truth there. He cupped her face in his hands. "I love you, Winifred Bellamy. I love your passion for life and your unflinching courage. I love the way your body welcomes mine. I love how you met my family and fit right in and saw past the craziness to the bond we all share. You're part of that now. Wolff Mountain claimed you. I'm claiming you. Say you'll marry me. We can wait six months or a year. If it will make you feel better about things. But I won't change my mind."

"What if I just say yes because I want to be part of your big, wonderful wolf pack?"

"Are you saying yes?" A grin spilled over his face.

"Perhaps."

"Then I think I could live with it. But I'd like to know, Winnie. For the record. Do you love me?"

Their gazes locked. Her pause bothered him more than it should.

Finally, she smiled through her tears. "You know I do, you wretch. Why else would I agree to have tree-house sex with you?"

"Is that anything like wild monkey sex?"

She laughed, her eyes wet and her cheeks flushed. "You tell me."

He kissed her long and slow, showing her what he was too clumsy to express with words. Winnie was soft and warm, and when her breasts nestled up against his chest, he felt his control slipping. "It's dinnertime. We can't do this."

She laughed, a wicked, knowing sound that made his breath catch. "Since when are you so worried about propriety?"

He gave in without much of a fight, following Winnie up the stairs to her unmade bed. "My family is never going to let me live this down."

She locked the door, stripped her shirt over her head and shoved him backward onto the bed. "I'll make it up to you, my love. I swear."

They wrestled like children, laughing and panting, ripping at buttons and zippers until they were both naked. He paused, his forehead pressed to hers. "Do you forgive me?" he asked, his throat tight. Surely she knew what he meant. Every stupid word he had ever uttered.

"Yes. Yes, I do. It's okay, Larkin. We're okay."

Relief was as sweet as spring rain. Settling his hips between her legs, he braced himself on his hands and looked down at her. "I didn't know," he said, shivering inwardly at how close he came to missing out.

"Didn't know what?" Her slow, quiet smile bathed him in peace, despite the fact that his body was taut with longing.

"I didn't know what it was that Devlyn and Annalise and my cousins had found. I thought I was different. More broken. That I couldn't have what they have."

She guided him into her center. The feel of her fingers on his rock-hard sex was heaven and hell. When he was all the way in, with their bodies locked breath to breath, he sighed.

Winnie's eyes were closed, a small smile curving her lips. "And what do they have, my wonderful Wolff?"

He flexed his hips, drawing a groan from her, a hiss of amazement from his own throat. "Love, Winnie. The Wolffs have love…."

Epilogue

Vincent Wolff lingered in the shadows, half-hidden behind a marble column as he surveyed the large room filled with people. Colors swirled in the form of handsome men and beautiful women dancing past his hiding place. The crowd included a few outsiders, close friends, but mostly family. Always family.

In the preceding eighteen months, he and his brother, Victor, had completed a massive addition to Wolff Castle, a wing off the back of the house that would help accommodate their burgeoning family. The new square footage included a small chapel, among other things.

Tonight, this magnificent ballroom in which he stood was being christened, filled and blessed with candlelight, laughter, music and dozens of white roses and calla lilies. Today was his son's wedding day. Larkin. And his bride, Winnie. Because their courtship and romance had happened so quickly, they had opted to postpone a formal wedding and in the meantime had enjoyed an extended engagement.

Though Victor had sensed from the beginning that Winnie could be a perfect match for his quiet, intense son, he had wondered sometimes if this day would ever come. Seeing the unguarded emotion on Larkin's face as his bride-to-be walked down the aisle soothed Vincent's fears. His boy had found love.

Devlyn had served as his brother's best man. Vincent had not been included in the wedding party. He had failed his children years ago, and the pain they had suffered left permanent scars.

After Devlyn's birth, Vincent's beloved wife had morphed into someone he barely recognized. Vincent had an idea why, but he had never spoken of it to anyone. And with God as his witness, he had never known the extent of her terrible, unspeakable break with reality until it was too late.

As it was now, the truth that caused her breakdown would never come to light. There was no reason. Life moved on. He was still paying for his mistakes. Telling what he knew would not exonerate him.

Some secrets were better off buried with the dead....

* * * * *

The saga of the MEN OF WOLFF MOUNTAIN *continues!*
Don't miss the finale that reveals
all of the Wolff clan's secrets....
Available October 2013.
Only from Janice Maynard and Harlequin Desire!

REQUEST YOUR FREE BOOKS!

2 FREE NOVELS PLUS 2 FREE GIFTS!

⬧ HARLEQUIN®

Desire

ALWAYS POWERFUL, PASSIONATE AND PROVOCATIVE

YES! Please send me 2 FREE Harlequin Desire® novels and my 2 FREE gifts (gifts are worth about $10). After receiving them, if I don't wish to receive any more books, I can return the shipping statement marked "cancel." If I don't cancel, I will receive 6 brand-new novels every month and be billed just $4.55 per book in the U.S. or $4.99 per book in Canada. That's a savings of at least 13% off the cover price! It's quite a bargain! Shipping and handling is just 50¢ per book in the U.S. and 75¢ per book in Canada.* I understand that accepting the 2 free books and gifts places me under no obligation to buy anything. I can always return a shipment and cancel at any time. Even if I never buy another book, the two free books and gifts are mine to keep forever.

225/326 HDN F4ZC

Name _____ (PLEASE PRINT) _____

Address _____ Apt. #

City _____ State/Prov. _____ Zip/Postal Code

Signature (if under 18, a parent or guardian must sign) _____

Mail to the **Harlequin® Reader Service:**
IN U.S.A.: P.O. Box 1867, Buffalo, NY 14240-1867
IN CANADA: P.O. Box 609, Fort Erie, Ontario L2A 5X3

**Want to try two free books from another line?
Call 1-800-873-8635 or visit www.ReaderService.com.**

* Terms and prices subject to change without notice. Prices do not include applicable taxes. Sales tax applicable in N.Y. Canadian residents will be charged applicable taxes. Offer not valid in Quebec. This offer is limited to one order per household. Not valid for current subscribers to Harlequin Desire books. All orders subject to credit approval. Credit or debit balances in a customer's account(s) may be offset by any other outstanding balance owed by or to the customer. Please allow 4 to 6 weeks for delivery. Offer available while quantities last.

Your Privacy—The Harlequin® Reader Service is committed to protecting your privacy. Our Privacy Policy is available online at www.ReaderService.com or upon request from the Harlequin Reader Service.

We make a portion of our mailing list available to reputable third parties that offer products we believe may interest you. If you prefer that we not exchange your name with third parties, or if you wish to clarify or modify your communication preferences, please visit us at www.ReaderService.com/consumerchoice or write to us at Harlequin Reader Service Preference Service, P.O. Box 9062, Buffalo, NY 14269. Include your complete name and address.

HD13R

SPECIAL EXCERPT FROM

 HARLEQUIN®

Desire

USA TODAY *bestselling author*

Kathie DeNosky presents

A BABY BETWEEN FRIENDS, *part of the series*

THE GOOD, THE BAD AND THE TEXAN.

Available July 2013 from Harlequin® Desire®!

They fell into a comfortable silence while Ryder drove through the star-studded Texas night.

Her best friend was the real deal—honest, intelligent, easygoing and loyal to a fault. And it was only recently that she'd allowed herself to notice how incredibly good-looking he was. That was one reason she'd purposely waited until they were alone in his truck where it was dark so she wouldn't have to meet his gaze.

The time had come to start the conversation that would either help her dream come true—or send her in search of someone else to assist her.

"I've been doing a lot of thinking lately…" she began. "I miss being part of a family."

"I know, darlin'." He reached across the console to cover her hand with his. "But one day you'll find someone and settle down, and then you'll not only be part of his family, you can start one of your own."

"That's not going to happen," she said, shaking her head. "I have absolutely no interest in getting married. These days it's quite common for a woman to choose single motherhood."

"Well, there are a lot of kids who need a good home," he concurred, his tone filled with understanding.

"I'm not talking about adopting," Summer said, "at least not yet. I'd like to experience all aspects of motherhood, if I can, and that includes being pregnant."

"The last I heard, being pregnant is kind of difficult without the benefit of a man being involved," he said with a wry smile.

"Yes, to a certain degree, a man would need to be involved."

"Oh, so you're going to visit a sperm bank?" He didn't sound judgmental and she took that as a positive sign.

"No." She shook her head. "I'd rather know my baby's father."

Ryder looked confused. "Then how do you figure on making this happen if you're unwilling to wait until you meet someone and you don't want to visit a sperm bank?"

Her pulse sped up. "I have a donor in mind."

"Well, I guess if the guy's agreeable that would work," he said thoughtfully. "Anybody I know?"

"Yes." She paused for a moment to shore up her courage. Then, before she lost her nerve, she blurted out, "I want you to be the father of my baby, Ryder."

Will Ryder say yes?

Find out in Kathie DeNosky's new novel

A BABY BETWEEN FRIENDS

Available July 2013 from Harlequin® Desire®!

THE SANTANA HEIR

by Elizabeth Lane

Grace wants to adopt her late sister's son. Peruvian
bachelor Emilio wants his brother's heir...and he wants
Grace in his bed. Can this bargaining–chip baby make
them a *real* family?

Look for the latest book in the scandalous
Billionaires and Babies miniseries next month!

Available wherever books and ebooks are sold.

HARLEQUIN *Desire*

ALWAYS POWERFUL, PASSIONATE AND PROVOCATIVE.

They're rich, eligible Texans… *Texas Cattleman's Club* is back in a brand-new nine-book miniseries!

TEXAS CATTLEMAN'S CLUB: THE MISSING MOGUL

Starting with *USA TODAY* bestselling author
Maureen Child's

RUMOR HAS IT

A strange disappearance rocks Royal, Texas, but for Sheriff Nathan Battle, mysteries of the heart take center stage when the woman of his dreams comes back to town….

*Available July 2013 from Harlequin Desire
wherever books and ebooks are sold.*

**And don't miss
DEEP IN A TEXAN'S HEART
by *USA TODAY* bestselling author
Sara Orwig in August 2013**

SADDLE UP AND READ 'EM!

This summer, get your fix of Western reads and pick up a cowboy from the PASSION category this July!

ZANE by Brenda Jackson,
The Westmorelands
Harlequin Desire

THE HEART WON'T LIE by Vicki Lewis Thompson,
Sons of Chance
Harlequin Blaze

*Look for these great Western reads AND MORE,
available wherever books are sold or visit*
www.Harlequin.com/Westerns

HARLEQUIN®

A Romance FOR EVERY MOOD™

Love the Harlequin book you just read?

Your opinion matters.

Review this book on your favorite book site, review site, blog or your own social media properties and share your opinion with other readers!

Be sure to connect with us at:
Harlequin.com/Newsletters
Facebook.com/HarlequinBooks
Twitter.com/HarlequinBooks